BURIED FAIRY

UNDERTOWN PARANORMAL MYSTERIES
BOOK 6

TABATHA GRAY

Author site: www.tabathagray.com

Editing by Victory Editing

Cover Design by Mariah Sinclair www.mariahsinclair.com

This book was written and is set in the traditional land of the first people of Seattle, the Duwamish People past and present. We honor with gratitude the land itself and the Duwamish Tribe.

AUTHOR'S NOTE

Did you know you can get exclusive messages from Undertown sent right to your email? It's like having a friend giving you the neighborhood gossip as you read.

If you picked up this book through my website, tabathagray.com, the bonuses will start arriving in your inbox just a day or so after your purchase.

And if you bought the book elsewhere, no worries at all! You can still get the read-along experience by visiting tabathagray.com/utbonus. Enjoy!

CHAPTER 1
MOON RIVER

he kettle screamed. Emma hurried to the stove and turned off the gas burner. The whistle died to a whimper. She carried the kettle over to her gleaming butcher-block counter and poured the bubbling water into two large white ceramic mugs with tea bags waiting. The steam that rose around her face smelled of ginger and lemons. On any other afternoon, she would have breathed deeply and let the comforting warm aromas drain the tension from her tight shoulders and invite her to take a quiet moment. But now she glanced nervously at the ticking clock above the kitchen door, then through the door itself into the hallway.

This time had to be different.

This reading had to go well, the client had to leave happy, and—most importantly—they had to actually pay Emma for her psychic services. Down the hallway came the sounds of wooden floorboards creaking. Emma's shoulders screwed tighter. The woman must have tired of sitting in the living room and had stood. What if she left before Emma even did her reading? She wouldn't be the first.

Emma jerked open her silverware drawer and grabbed a spoon, then scooped the soggy tea bags from the mugs and flicked them into the trash. She opened her little blue sugar well and tossed a spoonful of sugar into each mug, spilling half of it on the counter. Then she grabbed the sloshing mugs and headed down the hall.

The living room smelled faintly of smoke from the fireplace. Emma's client was looking through the large front window at Undertown Square's fall foliage. The woman seemed to be in her sixties and not afraid to show it. Silver streaked her black hair. She wore a navy cashmere cardigan over a crisp white silk blouse and tailored charcoal-gray slacks. The outfit screamed money.

"Sorry that took so long," Emma said, handing the mug of tea to the woman. Emma's stomach did the twist. In the presence of this wealthy client, the mug, even the entire room, seemed cheap and unpolished. Emma tried not to think of the pile of unpaid bills back in the kitchen. "Would you like to sit with me and tell me why you've come?"

"Something strikes me about this photograph." Her voice was low and throaty. She was staring at a small photograph hanging next to the window. "It's clear that you've put a great deal of thought into picking the white sofa and pairing it with the walnut side tables and the chair. Your choice in art might be pedestrian, but at least it is consistent. But one of these things is not like the others. This photograph simply doesn't fit."

Emma glanced across the room at the framed snapshot. She knew its subject by heart: a grainy, blurry, yellowed picture of a man with sideburns holding up a can of beer in front of a cherry-red motorcycle. "It's my dad."

"I suppose one can't choose one's family."

Emma felt a flush of heat creep up her neck. The last she'd seen of her dad had been at the Evening Palace. He had been trapped by the fae for over thirty years, hypnotized and forced to work as their servant. He'd run back into the collapsing palace to help save the others. Who was this woman to judge him? Emma bit back her annoyance. "You didn't come to ask me questions about my decor, did you? And I'm sorry, but I never got your name."

"That's because I never gave it to you. I'm not like the people who typically engage with providers of your type of services. I don't care to see what my future holds. I don't want to know if I will find love or lose love or if I will win the lottery."

"I couldn't tell you that anyway."

"Precisely! That is what the rabble can't understand. You are a specialist, and there is no one I love more in this world than a specialist. I don't want you to tell me about the future. I want you to tell me about the past. And you are, I understand, in a unique position to consult with entities who have knowledge of the past."

"But you won't give me your name?"

"I simply want to know who I'm working with before I give you any potentially compromising information. For you see, my family has a long history and an even longer reach. But we have our vulnerabilities, especially now. If our enemies learn we've resorted to—"

"Asking someone like me for help?"

"They would move to take advantage of our perceived weakness." The woman's painted lips spread into a smile. "I'm so glad we understand each other."

Emma fought to keep her face from turning into a scowl. Who did this woman think she was, coming into her house and treating her like an embarrassing little secret? Still, the pile of bills on the kitchen table got bigger every day. Her new psychic business hadn't exactly made her a millionaire. Even though she had the gift of contacting spirits, it never seemed to go as planned. Half the time she'd bring in the wrong spirit or an unhelpful spirit or a spirit with a score to settle. This reading had to be a success. She forced a smile. "Why don't we sit, and you can tell me what you need from me."

"Isn't that obvious?" The woman flashed an amused grin and strolled to the sofa. She considered it for a moment, then sat in a leather armchair.

"You want me to contact the spirits for you, but not for any pedestrian reason." Emma placed special emphasis on *pedestrian*.

"Yes, it's a matter of wills."

"A battle of wills? The will to succeed? The will to victory?"

"The will to an enormous estate." The woman's features sharpened to a point. "My father's, to be precise."

Emma's breath caught in her chest. She knew what it was like to lose someone you love. "I'm sorry—"

"Don't be. Father was a monster." She chuckled. "A very rich monster. My three brothers probably danced a jig when they received word of his passing. I know I did. Finally it seemed like we would all be free, free from his twisted schemes and his stormy moods, from his pettiness and cruelty. And moreover, we were rich! The only matter to be taken care of was to read the will to the family and see how we would share the spoils—there was plenty for all of us to live out our days in splendor."

"Must be nice."

"It will be."

"So the will reading didn't go as planned?"

"How could it? There was no will to read."

"In that case, doesn't the probate court—"

"For reasons that will become apparent, my family is unable to patronize such institutions. Besides, we know a will exists. Father told us about it constantly. He told the whole family. I should have known that it was just the prelude to another one of his twisted games."

Emma considered this information. The will was missing at the time of death, yet the father had told them all about it as a trick. She inhaled sharply. "He wants you to find the will."

"I see that your reputation might not be entirely undeserved. Father loved nothing more than bending others to his will, so to speak. I should have expected he wouldn't go gently into that good night. No, even though he's dead and buried, he still reaches out to control us, to pit us against each other, to keep us jumping. Well, I am tired of jumping. I would like to see the old man jump."

Emma saw where this was leading, and she wasn't sure she liked it. Most of her clients came to her to find solace from the departed, not to control them. "You want me to summon your father's spirit and force him to tell you where he hid his will."

The woman's eyes searched Emma's before she spoke. "Force is such a strong word, isn't it? Force requires a threat, yet how could I possibly threaten a dead man? When I said I'd like to see him jump, I meant I'd like to see the surprise in his eyes when he's dragged from his postmortem bocce ball court back to the real world to answer my questions."

It made sense even if it was a little weird. "You know you won't be able to see him yourself. Only I can see the spirits I call."

"Yes… of course." Her mouth slacked subtly, and her brow lowered. It only lasted a moment before her crisp demeanor returned. "But we are getting ahead of ourselves. Before we can summon my father's spirit, I have to know if I can trust you."

"Do you… want references?"

"References would merely expand the problem. How can I know if your references are trustworthy and not, say, three of your closest friends doing a favor?" She raised an eyebrow as if to say she knew all about favors. "I have a better idea, a test."

A cold sliver of doubt drilled into the base of Emma's

skull. A test? What was this woman's game? Why couldn't Emma ever get any normal clients? She tried to hide her doubt. "What kind of test?"

"Here." The woman held out a slip of beige paper folded in half.

Emma hesitated. What was she getting into? Still, she couldn't resist a mystery. She took the note, unfolded it, and frowned in confusion. The page contained a single name written in a spidery cursive, along with a lock of slick black hair fastened to the paper with clear tape. "Lenny Scaglione?" she read aloud.

"Summon him and have him answer my question, and I will know that you're worth the risk of revealing my name."

"What's your relation to this man?"

"Private."

Did this mystery woman expect her to contact a spirit with nothing more than a name and a piece of hair? And anyway, who just randomly carries around pieces of dead people's hair? This wasn't how readings normally worked at all. Normally, Emma contacted spirits intuitively from the bond they had with the client. It was a matter of reaching out and sensing the bond, then following where it led. But from the doubt, a question arose, flitted around, and poked the inside of her brain. Could she do it? Could she summon a spirit with so little to go on? If she managed it, maybe Lenny could give her some answers about the strange woman. Emma nodded to herself. "I'll try. Give me a minute."

Emma shifted and sat upright with her feet planted on the floor. She looked at the letter and the hair, and then she closed her eyes. Freed from the burden of mundane vision, she let her attention travel to the texture of the paper in her hand. It was thicker than ordinary note paper, and it had an expensive softness. Whoever this mystery woman was, she had money, but there are some things that money can't buy. One of them is the gift of the fae.

Emma directed her attention toward the gift and touched it. Like turning on a light switch, the world around her lit up. Though her eyes were still closed, she saw her living room, saw the fireplace and the sofa, and her hand holding the note. All these things were bathed in light from the countless silken filaments which connected her to them, which connected them to each other.

Looking at the dead man's hair, she saw a few dozen threads connecting it to her, and to the strange woman, and beyond. She reached out with her mind and ran her focus along the threads, plucking them like harp strings and feeling their vibrations. One strand caught her attention. It was nearly transparent, and it sounded like a sigh when she plucked it. She picked it up and tested it, checking its weight and strength.

The more she focused on the thread, the more she was convinced it would lead her to the former owner of the hair. She tugged it gently. It didn't break. She applied a stiff but steady pressure, and by inches it gave way and released, and she had the impression of something moving toward her faster than the wind from unimaginably far away.

A man's spirit materialized in front of her. He was handsome, with a nice tan and slicked-back hair. He wore a pink polo shirt with the collar popped and smartly creased chinos. He winced and put his palm on his forehead. Then he looked up and locked eyes with Emma. There was malice there. He lunged toward her. "Where am I? Who are you? And what's the meaning of this? I was playing the ninth with Big Jerry and was about to score a hole in one! And now you think you can come along and pull me out of my afterlife like I'm a nobody?"

"Hello, Lenny," the woman said in a cool monotone.

Lenny skidded to a stop. His eyes went wide, and he staggered back. If he hadn't been a ghost, he would have tripped over a side table trying to get away. Instead, he passed right through it and stood pressed up against the fireplace. The light from the fire filtered through his transparent body and cast twisted, writhing shadows onto the white rug. He raised a trembling finger and pointed it at the woman. "You!" His voice quavered. "You've got a lot of nerve."

"By our host's tortured facial expression, I gather that you have arrived and that you are no doubt hurling invectives in my direction. I will remind you of the oaths you made to my father. Oaths sworn in blood on the graves of your parents. Oaths binding even in death."

Fire raged in Lenny's eyes, but he remained silent.

"You will be happy to know that I have asked you here to answer a single question. Once answered, you may leave and go back to… heaven?" She chuckled. "Doubtful."

"Well, lay it on me."

The woman glanced at Emma, who nodded for her to proceed. "I want you to tell me what was our song. The song we danced to that night on the riverboat after everyone else went back to their cabins and it was you and me on the deck." Her voice caught. "You paid the band a G-note to keep playing that song over and over, and you said you'd never seen a moon so big or a girl so pretty. It was the last song we ever danced to before your accident."

"Accident?" Lenny chuckled. "Is that what they're calling it? What I don't understand is why you'd drag me all the way to this dump to ask a question you know the answer to. You know as well as I do it was 'Moon River.' It was always 'Moon River,' Linda."

So the woman's name was Linda. Emma turned to her and said, "'Moon River.'" She left out the other stuff.

The woman smirked. "Thanks for your help, Lenny. You can get back to playing the harp with Saint Peter or whatever you do to pass the time."

"Yeah, whatever," Lenny said as he faded back into noth-ingness. "Good luck. From what I hear, you'll be needing it."

Silence hung between them for years before the woman broke it. "Congratulations, Emma. You passed the test. You're the real deal. I expect that whatever I tell you in this session of ours will remain confidential."

"I never share my clients' secrets."

"What did I say? You're a specialist, a professional. You know the value of keeping your people happy." She reached into her purse and retrieved another small note. "This piece of paper contains the name of my father."

Emma took the note and unfolded it and read the name Leo Cappotelli. She closed the note and handed it back to the woman, who rose and tossed it in the fireplace.

Leo Cappotelli. Where had she heard that name before? It must have been years ago, on the news. There had been something about a trial. Emma remembered visiting her mom from college and glancing over to the always-on TV where the cable news showed someone in a dark suit on a perp walk. Fear uncoiled in Emma's stomach and rolled around like a black snake. She bit her bottom lip, then looked up at the woman, whose smile seemed suddenly predatory, feral. "Your father is Leo Cappotelli?"

"He was."

"And this would be the same Leo Cappotelli who's head of the Cappotelli crime family?"

The woman's laughter filled the room. After it died down, she regarded Emma with a smile. "He was."

CHAPTER 2
TARGET

Sassy, captain of the Night Watch, looked down on Undertown Square from his perch on the historic theater's roof. The air felt crisp in his feline nostrils. The spicy scent of fallen leaves mixed with the scents of coffee and pastries from the café below as well as the more appetizing scent of frying bacon from the diner. The long, sweltering summer was finally over, and he was grateful for the cool air. He had more than a hunch he'd be on the chase before afternoon turned into evening, and his black and-brown fur, however magnificent, did trap the heat.

He went over the plan again in his mind, the angles of approach, the escape routes. He'd drilled them incessantly, even though he knew Undertown Square like the back of his paw. Two years ago, when the place was still cursed, he and the rest of the Night Watch had been almost the only creatures who could slip past the magical barriers and enter this abandoned part of town. Those had been tough years, always skating on the edge of the abyss. But he'd never felt so free as he had when running along the desolate rooftops chasing or being chased by fell creatures. Now things were different. Or maybe Sassy was just getting old.

"Sector C locked down, sir," Kit said, approaching Sassy on the edge of the roof. She sat next to a pitted stone gargoyle, a horrible, unnatural thing full of wings and horns and teeth. Kit's radiant white fur made her look like an angel, but Sassy knew her better than that.

"Good work, Kit. That's the last sector. We've built the trap. Now we wait."

"How did you know that today would be the day?"

"A little bird told me."

Kit laughed. "And is the little bird still singing, sir?"

"Why Kit, I'm surprised. You know it's against Watch regulations to eat informants." He grinned. "I had a hunch about today. Barriers are always thinnest at the equinox. To make things worse, the humans in Seattle Above are having a festival with flutes and costumes and roasted meat and ordinary people pretending to be lords and ladies. They call it a Renaissance Faire."

"Sounds irresistible to the fae folk."

"They wouldn't miss the chance to slip someone into this world to repair the portal." Sassy looked down at all the civilians going about their lives, sipping coffee by the fountains, reading books, or playing with their kids. Sassy sighed. None of them knew how hard the Night Watch worked to keep them safe, to keep the whole world safe. They were lucky. "Hey, Kit, do you ever wonder what it would be like to retire?"

"What do you mean?"

"To say to blazes with all this and pack up and see the world."

"Who'd run the Watch?"

"Bill."

"He's all muscle and no brain. If you let him run the show, this place would be swimming in fae in no time."

"Then I could send to headquarters and get some kid fresh

from the academy. They really teach them these days. The kids know their stuff. Not like when we were cadets."

"Suppose you did retire. What would you do with yourself? I could barely stand watching you pretend to retire to draw out the Mockingbird."

"Like I said, I'd travel."

"You going to walk? Maybe smuggle yourself in some human's luggage on a flight? Or maybe you'd talk that human of yours into playing tour guide?"

"I spent some time in my youth riding the rails." It sounded more impressive than it was. When he was young and dumb, he'd jumped into a boxcar looking for a dry place to sleep, then woken up on the other side of the country. It boggled the mind to think of how his life would be different if he'd never seen that train.

"Do me a favor and save the tall tales for the kittens. We've got work to—" Kit swiveled her head. "Did you see that?"

"I did." Across the square, they saw two more quick flashes, like a fish glimmering in a creek. "That's the signal. Billy's spotted the target near the library. He's supposed to tail them, not pounce. You and I need to be careful not to give the game away. We'll go in quietly." Sassy padded across the roof and jumped onto some scaffolding. He looked over his shoulder and was happy to see Kit following close behind. "What do you think? Should we take the library tunnel?"

"That place gives me the creeps, but it's the fastest. Especially with all the people around."

"Let's do it then." Sassy threaded his way through the scaffold and jumped onto the pavement. They headed for the large municipal building to their right, slipped in through an open window, and found a staircase that took them to the basement and the tunnel below. It was a strange tunnel. The walls were made of red brick, and the ceiling was timber. Bare lightbulbs nailed to the walls emitted an orange, flickering light. Somewhere in the distance, water dripped.

"This is no place for a cat," Kit said, spitting out the cobwebs that had stuck in her mouth.

"It's better than it used to be. Those university types did us a real favor installing the lights." A team from the university had been hard at work mapping the tunnels for months. After losing a few undergrads, they'd installed lights and signage throughout.

"Ever since they opened that portal to the Evening Palace, the tunnels smell like the fae. Their stench is still here. Can't you smell it?"

"We've combed every inch of the tunnels. The portal's broken. The fae are gone."

"But not their stench."

Sassy sniffed and smelled nothing except dirt and mildew. A sliver of doubt needled his heart. Why couldn't he pick up the scent? He'd always been proud of his sense of smell. On a calm day, he'd been able to sniff a rat from a quarter mile away. Had that changed? Or was it only this particular odor that he couldn't detect? It was yet another way that his brief trip to the fae realm had changed him. "What… what does it smell like?"

Kit grimaced. "Cotton candy."

Maybe it wasn't so bad that he couldn't smell it after all. Few things smelled worse than cotton candy.

Up ahead, the tunnel branched. They took a left, then walked through a small arched doorway into the lower level of the library. A set of dusty, cold concrete steps took them past the darkened expanse of the lower stacks and up to a large room with enormous windows along its south wall.

A dozen humans sat at large oak tables. A man with a gray steel trolley weaved between the tables, collecting unused books. He looked at Kit and Sassy, blinked, and did a double take. "Who let in the cats?" he said to no one in particular. "Shoo!"

Kit growled. "Why, I ought to—"

"Forget about it, Kit," Sassy said, picking up his pace. "If you have beef with the humans, settle it on your own time. We need to stay focused. Do you remember the plan?"

"You never let me have any fun."

"Do you remember?"

"Yes, I remember! It's not like I didn't spend the past week studying it! We're in quadrant one. Billy gave a signal of three flashes. That means the target is moving east along vector twelve toward the broken fae portal. Vector twelve branches into three intersection points. We'll exit the library, see which way they're going, and intercept them before they can reach the portal."

"You make it sound like a walk in the park."

Kit grinned. "Easy as mice."

"I hope, for all our sakes, you're right."

They exited the library through the side door, which had been left open for them. Though it wasn't as high as their previous vantage point, the library's entrance overlooked the square below. Sassy squinted and scanned the field for any sign of Bill or their target. "I don't see them," he finally said.

"Me neither."

Sassy lifted his nose and sniffed. The scents were more complex here than they had been high atop the theater. Here the bold scents of coffee and bacon mingled with the smell of books, of the water in the fountain, of a thousand substances that he knew only by their aromas. He relaxed. His sense of smell hadn't completely left him. Suddenly Sassy's nose prickled. He sniffed again. A familiar scent. "Billy's here... He's close."

The bushes next to them shook, sending up a piney odor. From inside the bush came a yowl of pain. Then the bush seemed to spit a ball of disheveled tabby fur before them, along with a cloud of small leaves which fluttered to the ground like snowflakes. The enormous orange cat sprang to his feet and looked around wildly. He seemed to take in Sassy and Kit, and a look of panic flashed across his face. "C-Captain, I made contact with the target."

"You did what? You were only supposed to tail him."

"I tried, sir. I followed the plan to the letter. I signaled you, then I fell behind him, following at a distance so as not to give myself away."

"What happened?"

"The target, sir. He wasn't following the plan. I expected him to follow the vector and head to the tunnels, but he didn't. He doubled back. He was examining the houses one by one, and then suddenly he turned around. I didn't have time to hide."

"Did he see you?"

"He looked straight at me. His… eyes weren't like any cat's I've ever seen. They almost looked human. They looked through me. It was like he knew everything about me. I thought if I didn't make a move, I'd never get a chance, so I pounced."

"You pounced. And the target got away."

Bill looked at the ground. "Yes, sir."

Panic rose in Sassy's throat. Why would the target go off course? If the fae were coming to Undertown, there was one logical place for them to go. There were only so many portals where they could enter the world in their chosen form, then slip back to their world with their victims. If the target wasn't making a move for the portal, he had another goal in mind.

Sassy shivered. How could he have been outmaneuvered? Despite his years of experience, all his planning, all his determination to keep the fae out of this world? Well, the game wasn't over yet. If the fae weren't playing it by the book, then neither would he. And he knew Undertown like the back of his paw. "Kit, activate the dragnet."

Kit nodded, then lifted her head and let out a piercing yowl that filled the square.

"Boss," Bill said, "The humans are watching us."

"Let them watch. Maybe they'll learn a thing or two." Sassy locked eyes with a human who had stopped in front of the library steps and was gaping at the three cats. The human, his will overpowered, looked down, then swiftly walked away. Sassy's gaze drifted up and took in the row of houses and shops lining the east side of Undertown Square. "You said the target was looking at houses. What did you mean by that?"

"I expected him to make a beeline for one of the tunnel entrances, but he ambled up the east side of the square. He reminded me of one of those humans who dress in blue and carry the bags."

"The target reminded you of… a mail carrier?"

"Just the way he went from house to house, looking at each one real hard."

"And that's all the intel that you collected?"

Bill looked off into the distance and scowled. He only had so many brain cells, and it could be a real struggle for him to rub them together sometimes. "He was talking to himself."

"What did he say?"

"Nothing that made sense. It was just a number. He kept saying it over and over." Bill closed his eyes and grunted like he was lifting a car off a trapped kitten. "One… oh… two… four… That's it! I remembered! Ten twenty-four!"

Sassy's heart raced, and he felt each one of his wiry hairs stand on end. Ten twenty-four. It wasn't nonsense. It was part of an address. The address of the only person who had ever bested the fae. A person who had taken their gift, rejected their terms, and collapsed their house around them.

Ten twenty-four was Emma's address. Home.

CHAPTER 3
G-NOTE

Heat radiated off the fireplace. Beads of sweat formed on Emma's brow and hands. She had been too eager for autumn, too eager to light the first fire of the season. Now she fought to hold back the vertigo and the nausea that she always felt in stuffy, too-warm rooms. Or maybe Emma's dizziness was caused by the expensively dressed woman gazing at her from the armchair. A bona fide Mafia heiress.

The burning log popped. Fire flashed and bathed the room in otherworldly crimson light. Emma's heart raced. She pushed back into the sofa, wishing that she could disappear. She'd started out the session worried that she would foul up her reading and not get paid. But now she sat across from the daughter of a convicted killer. Emma wished she could call Viv or Riley and ask what to do. She wished she could use her gift and ask the spirits for guidance. But there was no time for that. She was on her own.

Okay. Step one. Stop. Freaking. Out. Think. She'd been in worse situations than this. In the fae realm, when hungry ghosts had drunk her life, was totally worse than this. And the present situation could have its advantages.

If this mystery woman's motives did turn out to be harmless, Emma could wipe out her pile of bills with the stroke of a pen on a checkbook. There'd be no more late nights worrying about the electric bill or money for a plumber. She wouldn't have to pick up odd jobs. She wouldn't have to borrow so much from her roommate, Viv.

There was risk here but also reward.

Still, Emma wouldn't use her powers for evil. No, she had to talk with this mysterious woman named Linda and learn something about her motivations and her goals. Then she'd make her decision. Emma set her jaw and locked eyes with the woman. "I don't want any trouble."

The woman sighed and suddenly looked tired. "And now you see the other reason I hesitate to give my name. It has this effect. It makes people back away, like they've stumbled upon a viper in the road."

"I didn't mean to—"

"Being a woman in the world is hard enough, but to be the daughter of Leo Cappotelli, butcher of Brooklyn. It's all anyone sees when they look at me. Do you have any idea how difficult that makes it to be your own person?"

"No—"

"Just because my father settled disagreements with cement boots, with piano wire and horse heads, doesn't mean that I work that way." She smiled sadly. "You and I are different, but I felt a kinship with you when I saw the tattered photo of your father on the wall. I don't know anything about him, but I recognize the struggle to reconcile the father with oneself. My own father, a violent, petty monster, fits into my life as much as that man with his grease-stained tank top and can of beer and motorcycle fits into yours."

Emma froze, her face a mask of confusion. The last thing she had expected from the woman was this sudden vulnerability and a rapier thrust to the heart. With great effort, she shook away the paralysis. "You say your father was a violent man, but you want me to contact him?"

"It's the only way. I hired a dozen of the best private investigators to find the will. I have an entire law firm scouring his papers for any clue. I even paid a team of forensic cleaners to pick apart his offices. None of them has produced the smallest lead. Believe me when I tell you that you are my last choice. I wouldn't have come here if I had any other options." The woman looked over at the fire. She seemed unaffected by its heat. "Perhaps you're surprised?"

"I mean, I wouldn't rank myself last…"

"I have always done things by the book. I have gone to the best schools, worked at the most prestigious companies, founded my own companies. I have rejected my family's old ways as barbaric and unprofitable. Unfortunately, my brothers…" She inhaled sharply. "My brothers are worse than our father ever was. If they inherit his fortune, they will use it to further enrich themselves at the cost of untold suffering."

Could the woman be telling the truth? Her aloof, self-contained expression had softened. She seemed sincere. But if Emma had learned anything since moving to Undertown, people weren't always what they seemed. "If your brothers are so bad, what makes you think that they would respect the terms of a will? You've said your family can't use the court system. Why won't your brothers simply take what they want?"

"The family has its own ways of adjudicating. If my father's will is brought before them, they will ensure that his wishes are carried out. They are bound to him."

Just like Lenny was bound. What kind of oath still held beyond the grave? Emma bit her lower lip and thought about the situation. She was starting to believe that the mystery woman was speaking in earnest, but the situation was so complex. "What if the will goes against you? If it gives everything to your brothers, then finding it will only make the situation worse."

"It would, but I believe it favors me."

"Why?"

She smiled sadly. "I was always Daddy's favorite."

A chill ran down Emma's spine. "Assuming I do help, what happens to me?"

"I'm prepared to compensate you magnificently."

"I'm not talking about money. What if your brothers decide that I'm to blame for their disinheritance?"

"I see. You are worried about your safety. I will grant you there is some risk. However, I believe that risk is mitigated by certain factors. First, I have no intention of revealing our relationship to anyone, let alone my brothers. Second, my brothers might be monsters, but they are practical and—to put it bluntly—you are poor. While they might get some satisfaction from taking out revenge on you, it wouldn't improve their situation."

"You're a real confidence booster."

"One must look upon the world with clear eyes no matter how unsavory."

"Thanks for the tip." Just what she needed. Motivational quotations, Mafia-style. Did they have posters hanging up in the garage where they mixed the cement? "Is there a third reason I shouldn't worry?"

"Yes. If my brothers decide to start a war against the family, they're likely to face problems greater than revenge. Problems of an existential nature."

"You would hurt them?"

"They will make their decisions, and the family will deal with them appropriately. Even if I threw myself on the ground and begged for mercy, it wouldn't matter. The laws that bind the family are ancient ones. My desires are irrelevant."

"With all due respect, it sounds like your family is even

more dysfunctional than mine. Let's say for the sake of argument I did decide to help you, explain to me what you want. Would I contact your father and ask about the will?"

"That would never work. One doesn't merely ask Leo Cappotelli questions and expect simple, straightforward answers."

"What would I say then?"

"First, apologize for intruding on his rest. Next, introduce yourself using your full name and explain that you have contacted him on my behalf."

"Do you think he'll be angry? Lenny was."

She looked toward the fire wistfully for a moment, then her eyes hardened. "Lenny was an idiot. He wanted to be a big man. It blinded him to opportunity. I don't think my father will be angry. I think he'll be intrigued. He's likely bored as sin in the afterlife and will jump at the chance to play his old games, to have another roll of the dice."

Emma suddenly felt sad for this strange woman. It was one thing to lose your father like Emma had. It almost seemed worse to have to walk on eggshells your whole life. Whoever this woman really was underneath the mask, she had to be exhausted. "So what should I say if I can't ask him about the will directly?"

The woman smiled. "It's simple. Tell him the wolves are circling and I need to know what to do."

"That's it?"

"I'm prepared to pay you ten times your normal rate, no matter what the outcome. In fact, I'll do that now." The woman twisted open the clasp of her ruby-red handbag and extracted a stack of hundred-dollar bills. She counted off ten of them, leaned over, and placed them on the coffee table in front of Emma. "If your conversation with my father results in the inheritance running my way, I'll be back with a bonus a hundred times as large."

"How will I know if it goes your way?"

"I'll tell you."

"How do I know if I can trust you?"

"I'd be a fool to burn bridges with someone with your skills. I don't know when I might need you again."

"Practical."

"Indeed."

Emma eyed the cash on the table. The bills were so crisp they might have been fresh from the mint. For the first time in months, she felt hopeful about her psychic business. A thousand dollars. In Lenny's parlance, a G-note. It wouldn't fix everything, but it would keep her afloat for a few more weeks. And if that bonus came through, everything would change.

True, the situation was sketchy, but there didn't seem to be any harm in contacting the woman's father. He was a spirit, and as much as spirits might frighten the living, they couldn't touch them, let alone hurt them. The brothers were scarier, but it seemed unlikely that they would ever find out about Emma. She turned to the woman. "I'll do it."

"Wonderful. Now allow me to introduce myself properly. My name is Linda Cappotelli."

"I know."

CHAPTER 4
DOOM

Sassy's paws pounded the damp grass as he ran toward the house. The wind flattened his whiskers. His ears were back and his fur bristled, but joy sang in his heart, the joy of the hunt. With Kit beside him, it felt like the old days were back, like he was young and spry and looking for action.

So far, there'd been no sign of the target. Just a handful of humans staring slack-jawed at the cats tearing through the park. Sassy's eyes darted from place to place, inspecting potential hiding spots, a maple tree's bushy red foliage, a row of garbage cans emptied and waiting to be brought in, the space under a big blue mailbox.

His gaze caught on something. Two green dots where they shouldn't have been. Eyes. Sassy skidded to a stop.

Kit shot past him, then called back over her shoulder. "What is it?"

"Quick, behind this tree!" He ducked behind the maple's slender trunk. "Over there, in the storm drain."

Kit peeked. "Something's looking out of the drain. Are you sure it's our target? Those don't look like cat eyes."

"Bill said the target had strange eyes. Remember, the

target's not really a cat. Not while that… thing is controlling him."

Kit muttered a curse under her breath. Sassy knew how she felt. Without a portal, the fae could only enter this world by possessing the body of a cat. The target was one of these unlucky souls. Though the fae could only ride a cat for a couple of hours, when they left, the cat would be changed. That's why it was so important to find the target. Not only to stop the fae from completing his mission but also to be there to help the poor cat adjust to his new world.

Sassy peeked out from behind the tree. The green eyes still looked out from the storm drain, scanning the park for something. Suddenly they swiveled and locked on Sassy's. The eyes went wide, then disappeared into the dark.

"We've got a runner," Sassy said. "You ready for a chase?"

"I'm always ready," Kit purred. She tensed, sprang, and became a white blur.

Sassy started a moment after and caught up with her at the storm drain. The concrete rubbed against Sassy's stomach as he squeezed through the opening.

He leaped down into the drainpipe, his paws squelching in the thin layer of mud. The air was humid and rich with the scents of dirt and mildew. The drainpipe stretched far ahead. The only light came from the storm drains placed every few hundred feet. They let in dim columns of light that flickered every time someone walked by above.

The target was not visible. He might have exited through one of the other drains, or he might have been hiding in the shadows, waiting to make his move.

Suddenly a gray tail streaked through one of the columns of light. Sassy's coiled muscles sprang into action, and he was on the chase even before he consciously understood what he'd seen.

The light from the storm drains strobed overhead as Sassy sped through the drainpipe. The flashing light made it impossible to see if he was gaining on the target, but no fae could work a cat's body as well as a real cat. They were liable to be slow and clumsy.

Ahead, the path branched. Sassy skidded to a stop. Kit joined him.

"Should we split up?" she asked.

"Wait." Sassy lifted his nose and sniffed. The target's odor was easily discernible over the background of damp humus. But he couldn't tell from here which path the target had chosen. He decided to try another approach and cocked his head, pointing his ear down the tunnel to the left, then to the right.

There. A faint scratching.

Silently, Sassy nodded toward the tunnel to the right. He and Kit began down it cautiously. The scratching sound got louder, and as they approached, Sassy heard something else. A quiet mumble, a pathetic, panicked kind of voice. "One. Zero. Two. Four. One. Zero. Two. Four," it repeated.

Silently Sassy approached the source of the noise. It was the first time he'd seen the target up close. The target was a pudgy gray-and-white cat, likely with some Persian blood. He had tried to exit the storm drain but was stuck. His rear end protruded into the drainpipe while his back legs scrambled to push him through.

"Looks like you've gotten yourself into a jam." Sassy laughed.

The target stopped his recitation, paused, then worked his back legs even faster, trying to escape. But the drainpipe's smooth concrete interior gave him no leverage. He must have realized it wasn't working, because he stopped pedaling his feet and started wriggling like a worm, trying to slide his chubby belly through the narrow opening.

"Will you stop it? You're embarrassing yourself."

"My only embarrassment," the cat wheezed, "would be to fail the prince!"

"You fae are always so dramatic," Sassy said. "But unless the prince sent you here to clean the drains, it seems like your little mission is over. By my reckoning, you're trapped in that poor cat's body for the next hour or so. Since you're just hanging around, I figured we could have a little chat."

"There's no time!" The target wheezed. "A doom has been placed upon the princess!"

"And I'd love to hear about it. Now, would you like to have this conversation with you stuck in the storm drain? Or should we pull you out and have a face-to-face? Of course I'd need a binding vow that you wouldn't try to escape. I understand you people take your vows pretty serious."

"You're offering to free me from this infernal trap?"

"I am."

"Well then…" The target's words fell into a mumble.

"What's that?" Sassy said.

"It's just so difficult to speak while being so squeezed. I said…" Again with the mumbling.

"Will you speak up?" Sassy stepped closer.

That was his mistake.

The target kicked with his back legs and they both found purchase against Sassy's forehead. Sassy braced against the force. It was enough to push the gray-and-white cat the rest of the way through the opening.

Sassy blinked up at the light where the target used to be. Anger flared in his chest, mixed with shame. He glanced at Kit. "Not a word of this to the team."

Kit swallowed her laughter. "Are you sure? I thought it was kind of heroic how you let him use your face as a booster pad."

"Not a word." Sassy scrambled up the side of the drainpipe and squeezed out of the opening. Soon Kit was beside him, the white fur around her legs matted in brown mud. The storm drain had landed them on a narrow side street bordered by brick and stucco townhouses. The sky had begun to mist. It felt cool on Sassy's face.

"Where did he go?" Sassy said.

As if in reply, there was a long moaning squeal of metal rubbing against metal. Sassy looked up and saw the rust steel staircase of a fire escape lowering. The target ran up the steps with a confused expression. He probably wondered why he wasn't getting any higher even though he was climbing the stairs. The fae probably didn't have counterweighted fire escapes.

Sassy and Kit jumped the fence and waited for the stairs to swing low enough, then they jumped on board. The pitted metal of the stairs scraped against Sassy's paws as he sprinted up them. At the top was a kind of landing next to the roof. It sounded like a kettledrum as they leaped onto it and then leaped away onto the roof ledge.

It was a flat roof, covered in black asphalt and slick with glistening mist. The target was three-quarters of the way across the roof. He jumped up to the ledge and looked over his shoulder at his pursuers. Then he jumped the narrow gap to the next building and kept running.

"There are only a few more houses on this block. Once he reaches the end, he'll have nowhere to go," Sassy said, leaping to the next roof. He veered around a skylight, past a wire shelving unit full of potted plants, past an AC condenser, then jumped another gap.

This was the life. The wind blowing in your fur. The song of the chase singing in your heart.

He saw the target now, on the last roof of the block, circling it, frantically looking for some way down. But this building didn't have a fire escape. There were no neighboring roofs to flee to. It looked out over the street and beyond to Undertown Square with its orange-and-red maple trees.

Sassy leaped onto that roof and heard Kit land behind him. He was breathing heavily, but the chase had given him energy instead of draining it. "That was fun," he called out. "But your little escape ends here. You're cornered in more ways than one. Look down at the park. You'll see several cats converging on this house, including a musclebound tabby that you gave the slip earlier. I imagine that he has a score to settle."

The target quickly glanced over the edge of the rooftop, then scowled.

Sassy still felt where the target's claws had bitten into his skin, but that hurt less than his pride. "We're going to take it easy and slow. I want you to walk to the center of the roof and lie on your back."

"You don't understand," the target called back, his eyes wild with panic. "I serve the prince, and I must deliver a message to the psychopomp!" He jumped onto the ledge, locked eyes with Sassy, and stepped into the void.

Sassy's heart did a somersault. It couldn't be. He sprinted to the edge of roof and hopped onto the ledge. That word, *psychopomp*, gnawed at him. Hadn't that been what the fae called Emma that night before they almost killed her? He didn't want to look over the ledge, but this was his job and he'd learned long ago to look reality dead in the eyes, no matter how ugly it got.

Sassy looked… and saw the target, still alive, hanging by a single claw onto a first floor awning. The target's grip gave way, and he fell into a bush, kicking up a plume of leaves. A moment later, the target emerged, a little unsteady but otherwise fine. He looked up at Sassy, then ran north.

"I'm getting too old for this," Sassy said, eyeing the awning.

"You and me both," Kit replied.

"Watch out, Kit, you're giving me hope. Maybe one day I just might convince you of the joys of retirement."

"Fat chance, sir."

"A cat can dream, can't he?" Sassy winked at Kit, then

jumped off the roof. He hit the awning at just the right angle to bounce him forward and let him land on his feet. It was a big drop, especially on the slick road, but his academy training had served him well. He sprinted after the target and caught up with him a block later. Sassy sprang onto the target's back, and they rolled together, a single mass of fir and claw.

It would have been easier if Sassy could have used his claws and teeth, but he held back. He didn't want to hurt the poor cat any more than the fae already had. But his restraint put him at a disadvantage, and a moment later, he found himself on his back with the fae target standing over him.

"I ought to pay you back for your impertinence," the target said, his eyes glinting with malice. Then the eyes shifted. He looked past Sassy and blanched. Kit and four other cats hurtled toward them. "But I serve the prince!" He turned and sprinted away, toward a yellow Victorian town-house with a rocking chair on the small front porch and an address plate reading 1024.

CHAPTER 5
DEAL

The room was still hot and stuffy. The mysterious woman who had introduced herself as Linda Cappotelli sat across from Emma with a self-contained intensity— No, Emma decided, it was fear. This woman had sought out Emma, given her an elaborate test, laid a pile of cash on the table, and asked to speak with her dead father. But now that the time had come, Linda looked terrified. It sent shivers down Emma's spine despite the heat. Could Linda really be that afraid of her own father?

From outside came a distant crash and yowling.

"What was that?" Linda bolted from her seat and looked around wildly.

Okay, this Linda woman was seriously on edge. She jumped at every little sound. Emma stood and walked over to her big front window and peered out onto the fall after-noon. A mother passed by, holding hands with a small child. They'd apparently decided to match because they both wore denim jackets and had their hair in braids. She wished she was out there with them, enjoying the crisp breeze. It was a shame the window sash had been painted shut. She turned back to Linda with a reassuring smile. "I don't see anything. It's probably just some animals. Are you okay?"

Linda touched her hand to her heart and let out a deep, juddering breath. "For a moment I thought— No, I won't trouble you with my problems." She grew silent, but her face told the tale of a woman struggling to master her emotions. She seemed to come to some conclusion and nodded to herself. "I'm ready to proceed. Do you remember my instructions?"

"Yes," Emma said, returning to her seat. The instructions. Was every Mafia family so formal? "I'm ready to begin."

She hoped it wasn't a lie.

Emma closed her eyes and sank into her power center. As she breathed in and out, the world fell away and she felt the tension drain from her shoulders, from her neck, and from her jaw. The threads lit up around her like fairy lights, and she saw the world and the connections between all things.

As she sank into deeper awareness, the stuffy room fell away. The space she now inhabited smelled like the forest after the rain. How hard could this be? Linda's father might have been formidable in life, but now he was a ghost, a shadow. After all, she contacted Lenny so easily, using only a name and a lock of hair. This time she had much more to go on. And if she was going to summon Linda's father, then the only logical place to seek him out was Linda herself.

Emma reached out with her mind, saw Linda, and immediately recoiled. She wished she could shield her eyes, but the light that blinded her wasn't in the real world. Once her eyes adjusted and she realized what she was looking at, Emma gasped. Where most people might have thousands of glowing silken threads connecting them to others, Linda had millions, maybe more.

What did it mean? She didn't know, but she was sure that somewhere in that mass of connections, there was a thread leading to Linda's father.

Emma began sorting through the threads, testing their weight, plucking them and listening to their particular frequencies. She couldn't have told you how long she kept at it, but after some time, she began to feel like she was peeling off layers of an onion. The threads at the outer layers concealed something unseen within. Emma suddenly knew what she had to do.

She plunged her focus right into the middle of the strands. They gave way, and she moved by feel, testing the texture of each strand. Some of them were coarse, some smooth, some felt like the shadows in the basement or the smell of fresh-baked cookies. None of them, however, felt right.

Then she found it.

One strand was thicker than the others, thick as a rope and tight as a violin string. It was unlike anything Emma had ever seen before. It pulsed with arcane energy.

Carefully she plucked the strand and heard gunfire, moaning, glasses clinking. It gave off the odor of brimstone and the impression of being unimaginably cold.

Carefully Emma tugged on the strand. Then it tugged back.

Her stomach jumped, and her heart raced as she gasped for breath. She wanted more than anything to let go of the strand, but she was stuck, frozen. It felt like when she almost drowned at the wave pool when she was nine. No matter how hard she tried to swim, the churning water dragged her under. She forced herself back to the present. She'd survived that day in the pool, and she would survive this. She was Emma Barrow, and she possessed the gift of the fae.

Before, Emma had only lightly tugged on the thread, testing it. Now she put the whole weight of her concentration behind the movement. She braced herself and pulled like she had never pulled before.

The thread pulled tight. The spirit resisted, tugged, tried with everything it had to outmuscle Emma, to resist her call, to stay in death. Sweat formed on Emma's brow. A splitting headache blossomed between her eyes. Yet she did not waver, and after only a few moments, she gained ground. The spirit gave an inch. Then another. Emma had won.

She dared to open one eye. Around her in the room swirled green, crackling ectoplasmic clouds. Linda sat plastered to her chair, eyes wide open, like she could sense the swirling energy, sense her father.

Emma pulled harder, and the clouds swirled faster. Its vortex tightened until it looked like an icy waterspout spinning in the middle of the living room. She pulled again. The vortex became a white blur and formed into the rough shape of a person. A moment later, the vortex disappeared. In its place stood a small, swarthy man in his midsixties. His thin black hair was slicked back, and he wore a smartly tailored black suit. He floated an inch above the floor and looked at Emma with small watery eyes.

Emma knew her lines. "My name is Emma."

The spirit of Leo Cappotelli looked at her with those cold, dead eyes. They reminded Emma of a dead fish's eyes and were utterly devoid of humanity.

"I apologize for disrupting your rest," she said.

The spirit remained utterly silent. Strange. Most spirits were chatterboxes when you summoned them. They might not be happy about being summoned, but they still talked a blue streak. Could he be waiting for her to finish?

"I am contacting you on behalf of your daughter Linda."

The spirit's eyes swiveled toward his daughter but didn't betray any hint of emotion.

"She instructed me to ask you what you wish her to do."

The spirit of Leo Cappotelli nodded, as if it was the most natural thing in the world for his daughter to ask him for orders, even beyond the grave. As if it were his place to give orders and everyone else's to take them.

Emma leaned forward in her seat. She glanced at Linda, who vibrated with anxiety.

The spirit opened his mouth to speak... Then a loud, sharp crash filled the room. A cool gust of air rushed past Emma, followed by a gray animal that scrambled over her feet and through the door into the hallway.

Adrenaline suddenly started pumping. Emma jumped up and spun toward the noise, but she couldn't comprehend what she saw.

Her large front window, the one overlooking Undertown Square, was fractured and splintered. Most of the bottom pane was missing, and large jagged glass shards protruded from its edges. Through this hole jumped a series of cats, one after another. They landed heavily, then tore after the gray thing.

Linda, her face a mask of terror, clutched her ruby-red purse to her chest and ran past the coffee table and through the front door, her navy cardigan fluttering behind her.

As if they were waiting for the sound of the slamming door, a wild cacophony of sounds came from the kitchen. It sounded like every pot and pan and plate and bowl was being thrown onto the floor at once. It was so loud that Emma almost didn't hear the noise behind her.

Her nerves singing, Emma spun around to find Sassy carefully stepping around shards of broken glass. "What the heck is going on?" Emma said to the cat. It wasn't a rhetorical question, and she wasn't crazy. Ever since she and Sassy had escaped from the fae realm, they'd been able to talk to each other.

"Watch business," he said without stopping.

Emma followed him to the doorway. "I need an explanation. Whatever's going on became my business the moment you and your friends crashed through my front window and scared off my client!"

An enormous tabby trotted up to Sassy and let out a series of low meows.

Sassy nodded. "Excellent. That closet has no way in or out except for the door. Keep the target there, and I'll interrogate him."

Emma watched the tabby turn and walk back toward the kitchen. "And now you have someone trapped in my pantry?"

"Not someone, something. Like I said, it's Watch business. Give me one hour, two tops, and we'll be out of your hair."

"What about my window?"

"I'll help you fix it."

"You don't have opposable thumbs!"

"Don't rub it in."

"What about my client? I was in the middle of a reading!" Emma remembered the spirit of Leo Cappotelli and quickly scanned the room but saw no trace of him. At least Linda left the pile of cash, although there was something else, a coin on top of it now. Where had that come from?

"Look, Emma, I'm not withholding information from you because it's fun. I'm doing it because it's safer for everybody," Sassy said, walking toward the kitchen.

Emma followed him. "Don't you think that I'll be safest if I know what's going on?"

"No."

"How am I supposed to protect myself if I don't know what the threat is?"

"You're not. That's my job."

"Just like you kept me from being kidnapped and taken to the fae realm?"

"That's a low blow. You know I did everything within my power—"

"But it wasn't enough! The only reason we ever made it home is because I figured out how to destroy the fae palace."

"Funny, I thought the only reason we got home is because a couple of your friends rescued you."

"It was a team effort!"

"Sure it was."

They entered the kitchen, where six of the toughest-looking cats Emma had ever seen were milling around the pantry door, conversing in a complex sequence of mews and growls and hisses. Something pounded on the pantry door from the inside.

"And that's exactly why you should tell me what's going on! After all, it's my pantry. I deserve to know what you've trapped inside it!"

The pounding stopped. A thin yet refined voice said, "Is that really her?"

"Is that who?" Emma asked.

"It is her! Blessed be! The psychopomp has arrived. Hark! It is I, your humble servant, Gresill. I come bearing a message from the prince!"

Gresill? Heat crept up Emma's neck as anger flared in her heart. Gresill was the fae who had led her to la danse macabre —the dance of the dead—where she was to be the main course for a thousand hungry ghosts. Gresill was the fae who so casually informed her that her power came at the cost of her father's freedom. A bargain struck hundreds of years before she was born. And now Gresill had broken through her window into her home, the one place in the world where she felt safest!

Sassy was right. There was nothing this monster could say that would interest her in the slightest. She turned to walk out of the kitchen.

"I hear footsteps," the voice in the pantry said, a note of panic ringing his voice. "Is the psychopomp still there? Tell me she is not walking away? By all the creatures that stalk the night, she's not leaving? Speak! Someone let me know! I must not fail the prince!" Gresill was silent for a moment, then his voice rang out again. "I am authorized to give you your heart's desire!"

Emma stopped midstride and looked over her shoulder at the pantry door. "And what would that be?" Despite herself, she felt curious.

"Oh dear," the voice muttered to itself. "What is it that humans want? To drink the blood of their enemies? No. To breach the well of boundless time and scoff at puny mortals?"

"I don't even know what that means."

"Really? I was certain that was it. Perhaps you could give me a hint?"

"There's nothing you have that I want."

"Not true. Definitely not true, if I can only remember what it is." The voice became tense and accusatory. "You must think, Gresill! Stop being such a dolt! Think like a human!"

"It's impossible," Emma said.

"Why?"

"You're not human. You're a monster. You kidnap people, take them from their families, and force them to work in your horrible palace!"

"That's it! I remember!"

"I'm not interested." Emma started to walk away.

"I am authorized to reunite you with your father."

Emma stopped dead in her tracks. "My father's alive? You have him?"

"Oh yes, yes. We most certainly have him. And we are prepared to reunite you with him in exchange for services rendered."

"I should have known there was a catch. What kind of services?"

"It's a task that I believe you will find quite agreeable. After all, it seems to be a hobby of yours if our sources are to be believed. His Highness has just been informed that Princess Isolde has had a doom placed upon her."

"Are you serious? The last time I saw your prince, he was chasing after me with murder in his eyes."

"Yes. I'll admit that His Highness was quite put out for some time. The Evening Palace, which you destroyed, was his sanctuary, his respite from the burdens of leadership, a place where he could let the burdens of the world fall away."

"The place was run by human slaves!"

"You say potato, I say potato."

"And now your prince wants me to save his sister?"

"You don't understand. The doom has been placed. Her life is forfeit. She is destined to be murdered before the clock strikes midnight. Saving her would be as impossible as changing the tides."

"Then what—"

"His Highness wishes you to be present at the scene and to find the killer."

CHAPTER 6
CALIGULA

Emma sat on her shoe bench and slumped back into the coats and jackets hung above it. They rustled and hissed and deflated slowly like a down pillow.

If only they could swallow her whole; then she wouldn't have to think about the fae in her pantry or the cats prowling her kitchen. She wouldn't have to taste the salt of the tears leaking from her eyes. She wouldn't have to think about the small framed photograph that she'd pulled from the wall and now gripped tightly in her hands: a grainy, blurry, yellowed picture of a man with sideburns holding up a can of beer in front of a cherry-red motorcycle.

She'd spent the past several months trying not to think about her ordeal at the Evening Palace. It had caught her by surprise. One minute she was confronting a killer, her own lawyer, in the middle of a public park filled with people enjoying the summer afternoon. The next minute she'd woken up in that palace filled with slaves and those awful fae. That alone would have been enough fuel to power a lifetime of therapy, but then, in the middle of it all, her dad appeared.

Emma had spent her whole life believing that her dad had

died in a motorcycle accident. It was a lie her mom told to shield Emma from a harsher truth. Her dad had gone out to the corner store one day and never returned.

Neither Emma nor her mom could ever have imagined he'd been kidnapped by the fae, hypnotized, and forced to work in the Evening Palace to pay off her family debt. For the contract that Alastair Barrow signed at the crossroads three hundred years ago.

Emma had learned all this over the span of an hour at a fae banquet where she was meant to be the main course. Was it any wonder that the whole thing seemed unreal? That she began to wonder if she had really met her dad? If she had really seen the Evening Palace collapse after he ran back in to help the other humans?

Was it any wonder that she'd pushed him out of her mind? Oh, it hadn't been intentional. But with bills and work and house repairs all crowding her attention, it was easy not to think about him much. And even if she had, what good would it have done? The portal to the fae realm was closed. Even if her dad survived the collapse, how could she have possibly helped him? He might as well be on top of Mount Everest or on the moon.

There was a knock on the door. Emma jumped. She shook off her thoughts, then stood and opened the door. When she saw who it was, she exhaled. "Thank God you're here."

"Like I'd miss the chance to see a third-party fae instantiation? Besides, we were just around the corner, finishing up mapping a new section of the tunnels." Riley grinned. They were a head shorter than Emma with messy blond hair and enormous round glasses perched on the tip of a pointy nose. You could have guessed they'd been mucking around underground because their oversized canvas coveralls were streaked with dirt. Riley cocked their head and looked at Emma. They lowered their brow and pulled their lips tight. "You've been crying."

Emma smiled and rubbed her eyes. When she'd first met Riley, she'd bristled at their directness, but now she'd come to appreciate it. Riley always had good intentions, even if their words were a little brusque. "I… I just need to talk some things out."

"Sure… Is it okay if my team starts documenting the phenomenon while we talk?" Riley gestured to three college-age boys roughhousing on the sidewalk. "They're house-trained. I promise."

"Yeah… sure." Emma trusted Riley implicitly. "Everything's happening in the kitchen. The fae's in the pantry. Your team can go set up in there. Just tell them to stay clear of the Watch."

"Oh, they know all about the Watch." Riley put their fingers to their lips and blew a piercing whistle. Moments later, the three research assistants were nodding respectfully to Emma as they passed through her hallway, carrying several large canvas bags toward the kitchen. Emma and Riley went into the living room.

"It looks like a hurricane came through here," Riley said, walking over to the broken front window. An autumn-scented breeze blew in.

"Be careful of the broken glass. It was crazy. They burst in here right when I was in the middle of a reading. I'd just summoned a spirit, and then the window exploded, and suddenly I had a three-ring circus rolling past me. And the awful thing about it was that the reading was going well for once." She felt sick. She'd been so close to earning that bonus! A spare hundred grand would have made life quite a bit easier.

"Did she pay?" Riley bent over and wiped their index finger on the floor. When they held it up to the light, its tip was the color of mud. They sniffed it. "I know you've had some problems with clients skipping payment."

Emma glanced at the coffee table. The pile of hundreds

was still there, thank goodness. But there was something else too, something that hadn't been there before. On top of the stack of bills sat a small shiny disk. She walked over and picked it up. "What's this? A gold coin? It looks pretty old."

Riley looked at the coin and let out a low whistle. "Not pretty old, really old. Ancient, in fact. I didn't know that coin really existed. I thought they made it up for the movie."

"What movie?"

Riley stared, slack-jawed, at Emma. "You mean you haven't seen it?"

"If I'd seen it, do you think I'd be asking?"

"Sorry, sorry, it's just that it's a classic. Considered one of the most influential movies of all time. Back in grad school, I used to have lunch with a woman in the film studies department. They taught a whole seminar about the symbolism of this coin in the movie."

"What movie?"

"*The Grandfather.*"

The room spun. Emma forced herself to focus. "That mobster movie?"

"Not that mobster movie, *the* mobster movie. It defined the genre and marked a transition from the more stylized movies of the fifties to the grittier, more realistic, method-driven movies of the seventies."

"Thanks, professor."

"You're welcome." Riley pushed up their glasses. "Assuming it's real, the coin you're holding is nearly two thousand years old."

Emma studied the coin. It had none of the mechanical precision that she was used to with modern coinage. It was lopsided, and its edges had been filed. The tail side of the coin depicted a chariot with the word *Roma*. The head side depicted a man in a toga with a laurel wreath. "Something about this guy looks off."

"It should. That's Caligula. The bloodiest emperor to ever

reign over the Roman Empire. He built a palace for his horse and forced Roman senators to run until they dropped dead."

"Sounds like he had issues."

"He did all those things to show that he had power, absolute power. In *The Grandfather*, the big mob boss has a coin just like this, one of two or three in existence."

"It's worth a lot of money, then?"

"It's priceless. It belongs in a museum. But in the movie, when the boss makes a big contract with someone, he gives them this coin."

"As payment?"

"No, as a promise that he'll be back to collect it. Because the thing is so valuable, anyone would be tempted to sell it. The only thing that prevents them is—"

"Fear," Emma said. Her mind raced. Had Linda left this coin? Had she thrown it onto the pile of bills on her way out? "Tell me, have you ever heard the name Leo Cappotelli?"

"Rumor was that the screenwriter of *The Grandfather* embedded in the Cappotelli family for a year before he wrote the script."

"I saw Leo Cappotelli today."

"But he just died— Oh." Riley had a faraway look. "Your client?"

"His daughter. She was trying to locate his will."

"And she left you this coin?"

"Either she did, or the spirit of Leo Cappotelli did." Yesterday she would have said the latter was impossible. Ghosts can't influence the physical world. But this ghost was different. He had tugged back, and for a moment Emma had felt her soul try to leave her body. Emma shuddered. "Just what I need, a Mafia princess and a fae prince after me."

"Tell me about the prince."

Emma walked to the side table where her canvas purse lay crumpled up. She pulled out her green faux-leather wallet, unzipped it, and placed the bills in the empty cash section.

After a moment's hesitation, she unzipped the wallet's built-in coin purse and dropped the priceless gold coin next to three dirty pennies and a tarnished nickel. She'd lost a lot of things throughout her life, but never her wallet. "He says that there's going to be a murder, and I have to solve it."

Riley frowned. "The stories and legends do hint that the fae look at time differently than we do. But even so, the fae rigidly adhere to their rules. If he asked something of you, he must be offering payment."

"My father."

"Oh."

"Do you think it's a trick?"

Riley shook their head. "No. The fae had a reputation for being tricksters, but they wouldn't invent a scenario out of whole cloth. They will adhere to the letter of any agreement they make but will attempt to trick you in the fine print. Of course if you enter into an agreement without reading the fine print, you could be in for a shock. What exactly did they offer you?"

"The messenger, Gresill, said that in exchange for finding the killer, he would reunite me with my dad."

"Do you see the problem with that offer?"

"I… No, I don't. It seems clear enough to me. I solve the case, and they bring my dad back to the real world."

"That's not what they said though! They said they would reunite you. They didn't mention anything about the real world. Maybe they plan on taking you back to the fae realm and reuniting you with your dad there. People talk about being reunited in death too."

Emma's heart pounded. "You think he's dead?"

"I don't know. Probably not. I'm just saying that you need to be very careful when making deals with the fae. There's always a catch, and they always extract the full measure of anything you've promised them."

"It almost makes me wish I had my lawyer." She would

have loved to have John Gruber look over this. He might have been mad. He might have convinced himself he was a changeling. He might have betrayed Emma and tried to sell her to the fae. But he was a heck of a lawyer. "I suppose I'll have to negotiate this deal myself. Will you help me?"

"Or miss the chance to document the inner workings of a fae pact? You couldn't keep me from helping you if you tried!"

"Okay, let me do the talking," Emma said. "If you see me screwing up royally, tap me on the shoulder and we'll huddle. We're going to negotiate this deal. I'll solve their murder, but only if they release my father back into the real world. No tricks, no strings attached."

CHAPTER 7

INVITATION

Emma stood in front of her pantry door. She felt the eyes of everyone in the room boring into the back of her skull. She looked over her shoulder. The floor was strewn with broken dishes. The air smelled strongly of peppermint from spilled loose-leaf tea. It was all too much. Did they really have to trash her kitchen?

Riley's team had set up five tripods at the far end of the kitchen by the stove. One held a camcorder. Another supported a small satellite dish that oscillated left and right. The rest of the tripods held bizarre, nonsensical items. A cage with a yellow canary. A red terracotta pot with a single tulip. A statue of Mary with a dark, viscous fluid leaking from her eyes. Did they carry all this around with them? It seemed ridiculous, but Riley was one of the world's leading applied folklorists, and if they thought this stuff was necessary, then it was.

The Night Watch clustered at the other end of the room from the students. A fluffy white cat groomed itself while the large tabby and several others paced nervously. The way they glanced between the pantry door and the students made you think they viewed both as equal threats. Emma wished she knew more about the Watch. Sassy went quiet every time she asked. He would tell her that the Watch's job was to keep the fae out of this world, but beyond that it was like talking to a boulder.

Emma faced the door again, reached out, and wrapped her fingers around the doorknob. The glass felt cool and slick. Her heart thundered. Gresill was behind that door, and just hearing his voice had brought back so many horrible memories. The last time she'd seen him, he'd led her to her doom. Now he was, somehow, locked in her pantry.

Emma scrunched up her nose. Wait a second. How could he possibly be trapped in her pantry? The Night Watch was formidable, sure, but Gresill was fae and taller than most humans. Why didn't he simply open the door and run? Come to mention it, why hadn't she seen him enter the house? Even though she had been busy summoning a spirit, she would have noticed something as big as a fae running by her.

She turned the doorknob. The latch clicked. The door shuddered. She pushed it open and was assaulted by a cloud of pungent garlic powder. A pair of glowing green eyes stared at her through the acrid fog. She froze, and as the fog cleared, she saw that the eyes belonged to a chubby gray cat cowering in the corner.

"That's a cat," She said, hoping someone would clarify. It most certainly was not Gresill, the ethereal fae consort she'd met at the Evening Palace.

"It's complicated," Sassy said, joining her in the doorway. "Without a portal, the fae can only enter this world by possessing someone else's body."

"But a cat?"

"Why not a cat?" Sassy said. He almost sounded hurt. "Cats have excellent senses. We're nimble. We're proud—"

"No, I get it. Cats are wonderful. But you told me the fae hated cats. Why would they choose to take a cat's body if they hate them so much?"

"We don't have a choice," Gresill said, finally finding his voice. "Believe me, I would rather suffer any number of mortifications before inhabiting a feline form. The senses, which you brag about, mean that odors, sounds, and tastes continually assault one's being. Instead of standing upright, I am forced to scurry along the ground. Instead of feasting on endless banquets at the royal palace, I am forced to eat spiders and mice and… kibble."

"Watch your mouth, fae," Sassy said.

"And do you have any idea how these creatures, ahem, relieve themselves? It's disgusting! When they informed me back at the palace, I thought it was all some bizarre prank."

Sassy growled. "Why I ought to—"

"Sassy, chill!" Emma said. "We're here to talk, not to brawl."

"As I was saying, I have no choice but to attend to you in this debased form. When the treaty of Croagh Patrick drove us out of this realm, it was specified that we might only return in feline form. I was elsewhere during the negotiation of that treaty, but my understanding is that it was a… joke. But I digress. Have you made your decision?"

"Let's talk about that. You offered to reunite me with my father. I would like to define that more precisely."

"How so? It's simplicity itself. You solve the murder by midnight tonight, and we will reunite you with your beloved pater."

"I've been told that your kind likes to sweat the details, so let's nail them down. In exchange for my services, you will transport my father to the front door of this house in exactly the condition he was when you took him from earth into the fae realm."

Gresill's green cat eyes glowed brightly. "That will be impossible. To return him to exactly the same state would mean making him young again. I'm afraid that is not in our power."

"Why not? He was young when I saw him at your palace."

"Not so much young as… preserved by the hypnotic bond which kept him in our service. The moment you broke his bonds, age descended upon him. Age can be delayed, but never completely deferred."

"Fine. Return him in the same condition except for his age. He will be in good health, with no curses, spells, bonds, or anything. Once you return him, then I will happily investigate the murder."

"We will be happy to deliver him in your house." He drew out the words strangely as he spoke.

Emma felt a tap on her shoulder and turned to see Riley shaking their head. It didn't make sense. Hadn't she wanted the fae to deliver her father? "Deliver." She turned the word over in her mouth. She remembered Gresill's odd phrasing. He'd offered to deliver her dad *in* her house, not *to* her house. And then there was the word *deliver*. He had pronounced each syllable separately. First *de* then *liver*.

Her blood ran cold. It was a trick! "No, you will certainly not de-liver my dad in my house. You will not remove his liver or any other organs!"

Gresill shrugged. "What a shame. It would have been fun."

Emma saw red. She charged into the pantry and towered over Gresill. "You think this is a game? You think this is fun?"

"W-what's wrong with enjoying your work?"

"You really are a monster, aren't you? My offer stands. I will investigate the murder. But first, you must transport my father to this house, healthy, happy, and unharmed in any way."

"What you ask is simply impossible. We cannot give without first receiving. It is written in our laws."

Riley whispered in Emma's ear, "They really can't."

"Fine," Emma said. "Then who decides if I've solved the murder?"

"Isn't it obvious?" Gresill said, with a twinkle in his eye. "If you solve the murder, then it will be solved."

"I may believe I've solved it, yes. But what if your prince disagrees?"

"Then your father will remain in our care."

"Unacceptable. I won't trust my father's life to your prince's whims. We need a neutral third party, a judge."

"Yet the victim is a fairy princess. No human court or judge can preside."

He was right. A human court would be too busy dealing with the whole *fairies exist* thing to try the case. But she didn't trust anyone on the fae side to deal in good faith. She needed to find someone whom the fae would accept but who was used to dealing with magical creatures. Wait a second! She knew someone who was intimately familiar with magic and who might have even run into the fae in her long life. "I propose Deidre Mallowan."

"The witch?" Gresill said. "Interesting."

Sassy stepped forward. "It won't work. She left town last week, and we don't know when she will return."

"Of course," Gresill said. "It is the equinox. She will want to be with her coven. I do wonder though— No." He laughed to himself. "Pardon me. I just had the most amusing flight of fancy about an impartial judge. At first, the idea seemed ludicrous, but the more I ponder, the more it pleases me."

"Out with it," Sassy said.

"I propose… you. Sassy, captain of the Undertown Night Watch, you will be our impartial judge."

Sassy scoffed. "Me? I'll tell you now, I'm anything but impartial. Why, I could just say that Emma solved the case right now and save us all the legwork. It's not like I care if some airy-fairy princess gets done for."

"I don't believe you'll lie to me. In fact, I have the utmost confidence in your honesty."

"Why? I have a thousand reasons to hate you."

"Because of the charter."

"Oh." Sassy looked down and muttered a curse.

"You remember the Night Watch Charter, don't you, Sassy? 'The Night Watch shall persecute and protect the normal world from all incursions of fae, spiritual, nocturnal beings' blah blah blah."

"Of course I remember it. You seem to know it pretty well for a fae," Sassy said.

"We have our own rules, the first of which is to know thine enemy. It's been some time since I read your charter, so forgive me if I paraphrase, but I believe the salient passage is 'Members of the Night Watch shall uphold the highest ethical standard in the line of duty and are forbidden from stealing, bearing false witness, et cetera.' Forgive me for pointing out the obvious, but—"

"I get it," Sassy said. "The charter keeps me honest even when dealing with the likes of you. Fine. I'll be your judge if Emma agrees."

Emma was still processing the fact that the Night Watch had a written charter. She'd always thought they were just a bunch of superintense cats who didn't like the fae. But even so, she couldn't imagine a better judge than Sassy. "I agree. If Sassy judges that I've solved the murder, the fae will transport my dad here, alive and unharmed."

"It would seem that we have reached an agreement. Let us shake upon it." Gresill lifted his right paw.

Emma hesitated, then bent and took the small paw between her thumb and forefinger. The cat's footpads felt dusty and soft. They shook.

"Now that we are agreed, allow me to inform you of the situation. The prince's sister, Isolde—"

"Let me stop you right there," Emma said. "The victim is the prince's sister, but you said she's a fairy."

"The fairies are, broadly speaking, the females of our kind."

"Like, the little guys with wings?"

"They aren't little, or guys, but they do have wings."

"I didn't see anybody with wings when I was in the fae realm."

"The Evening Palace is a… men's-only institution. Must we really waste time on such unimportant—"

"I'll decide what's important," Emma said. "Since you've come to me, I assume that the crime scene is somewhere nearby. But if she's fae, how did get here with the portal broken?"

"She's not a fae, she's a fairy. Different rules apply. Boundaries for them are not so rigid. But really, we must hurry—"

"No," Emma said. "I'm going to collect all the information I need. Sassy, what do you know about fairies?"

"Some fairies have been known to smuggle contraband between the realms but don't kidnap or enslave anybody. The Watch doesn't care about them."

"Thanks." Emma turned back to Gresill. "Now I want you to tell me where the crime scene is, and none of your tricks."

"I don't have time for tricks!" The green light from the cat's eyes dimmed. He frowned and closed his eyes, as if he was willing himself to perform some unpleasant task. Then he coughed. One wheezing cough followed another, and a moment later something hard and metallic clattered onto the floor.

Emma bent and examined the object. It was coated in fur and saliva, but she made out the outline of a silver crescent moon surrounded by a golden sunburst. At the top, there was a loop with a small golden chain threaded through it. "Is it a necklace?"

"Congratulations," Gresill said. His eyes were dimmer, he

panted, and he seemed to have difficulty standing upright. "You have all witnessed… the single most… humiliating act that I have ever… performed in duty to my prince." His voice was quiet now, almost a whisper. "This charm will grant you entry to the coronation, where it will occur." He curled up and tucked his tail over his front paws and closed his eyes.

Emma crouched next to Gresill. "What coronation? What will occur?"

When Gresill opened his eyes, they almost looked like normal cat eyes. They almost didn't glow at all. "Look for the harlequin, and…" He nodded off again.

"And what?" Emma put her hand on Gresill's back and shook him, trying to wake him. The fur was soft and warm. A moment later, the creature opened its eyes, and they no longer glowed at all. Gresill was gone.

CHAPTER 8
LET'S ROLL

"Meow?" the chubby gray-and-white cat said. It sniffed the air, and then its eyes moved back and forth, as though it was trying to figure out how it got into that stuffy room that reeked of garlic powder. It didn't seem scared, just confused. It stood and tried to stretch, but its knees buckled, and it landed back on the ground.

Emma sat on her knees next to the poor thing. It was so cute and so chubby and so pitiful. She forgot about Sassy and the Watch. She forgot about Riley, their assistants, and the strange machines on tripods. The cat's eyes no longer glowed. Its mouth no longer twisted to Gresill's cruel, playful smile. No trace of the fae remained, just a poor shaky kitty.

Without meaning to, Emma found that she had reached to pet it and run her fingers over the short, slick fur on top of its head, down its neck, and into the longer, fluffier, gray-and-white fur that covered its back. The cat lifted his head, rubbed it against her arm and purred.

"What just happened?" Emma asked the cat.

"Time ran out," Sassy answered, "The fae can only ride a cat for so long before the cat's natural warrior spirit evicts them."

Emma scratched the gray cat's cheeks, then moved up to its ears. "Warrior spirit?"

"You'll see it soon enough," Sassy said. "When the fae ride you, it changes you. It's a rude awakening. Previously, life was just naps and meals and chasing things that run. Now? Life is complicated. Our friend has just had his worldview expanded."

"Will he be okay?"

"The Watch will take care of him. It's what we do. It's who we are." Sassy looked over his shoulder at the team of cats standing in the pantry doorway. "Kit? Why don't you help our recruit find his feet and maybe a little food?"

The fluffy white cat detached from the group, walked over, and started grooming the confused gray cat. She used her tongue to smooth out its mussed fur, and she spoke to it in a series of low mews. A moment later, the gray cat stood. It was still wobbly but managed to make it out the door.

Emma watched them leave, and then her gaze fell on the sun-and-moon charm still lying in a puddle on the floor. She moaned, then stood and pulled a pair of latex gloves from the pantry shelf. They felt cool and rubbery as she put them on, but her hands soon started sweating. She picked up the charm and walked to the kitchen sink, covered it with soap, and scrubbed it under running water. Once it was clean, she unrolled a length of paper towel from the dispenser and set the charm on it to dry. "This thing is supposed to let me enter the coronation, and then I'm supposed to find the harlequin, whatever that means. Any ideas?"

"I'm drawing a blank," Sassy said. "Gresill is the fae prince's stooge. Maybe the prince is going to be crowned king?"

"That can't be it," Emma said. "A fae coronation would happen in the fae realm. He wouldn't need my help. No, whatever this coronation is, it's going to be happening right here in the real world. But how is that possible? We're in America. Not having a king is, like, our whole thing."

"Um, guys," Riley said, staring at the charm. "I recognize that design with the moon inside the sun."

"Well?" Emma said.

"I'll show you," Riley said. They went over to one of the canvas carryalls and pulled out a thin metal laptop. "Just let me connect to the Wi-Fi… and presto! Here you go." They turned the computer around for everyone to see. The sun-and-moon design was at the top of the screen. Below were photos of people in armor, of a minstrel playing a lute, of someone in a not-very-convincing dragon costume guarding a pile of papier-mâché gold.

After everything that she and Riley had been through, Emma had expected them to whip out some ancient illustration showing this very amulet worn by an Egyptian pharaoh, or maybe some worn-out treatise proving that the symbol was embedded in the Declaration of Independence by Thomas Jefferson. Whatever she had expected, it wasn't this. "The design on the necklace is the logo for a ren faire?"

"Not just a ren faire." Riley's eyes sparkled. "The Emerald City Ren Faire. It takes place each year at a large forest estate donated by one of the first Microsoft employees. It was founded in the eighties by a group of people who reenacted medieval jousts. Now it's the biggest faire on the West Coast."

"I'm sure it's impressive, but what does it have to do with the fae?"

"They love them," Sassy said. He sounded disgusted.

"Renaissance festivals might have started out as historical reenactments," Riley said. "But they've changed over time. Some people got bored with dressing up as knights, so they made robes and dressed as wizards. That escalated into drag-ons, then all kinds of mythological creatures. The Emerald City Ren Faire embraced the fantasy element more than others. Now you're as likely to see someone dressed up as a gargoyle as you are a blacksmith."

Sassy growled. "There's not too many places in this world where somebody with wings can walk around freely. And the music, the games, the drama, they're irresistible to anyone with a drop of wyrd blood. That's why ren faires are paranormal central, especially at the equinox. The barriers between worlds get thin. A lot of merchandise gets moved."

"Merchandise?"

"I mean that humans want anything they can't have. From that shiny red apple in the Garden of Eden to pixie dust smuggled in from the netherworld. What better place to move it?"

"And the Watch stops them?"

"Not our job."

"Great, so we have a fairy princess named Isolde who's about to be murdered at the ren faire. Gresill said she's doomed, that there's no chance of saving her, but I don't believe it. There's always hope. I'm going to go to the Emerald City Ren Faire and try to save her."

"We don't have a description," Sassy said.

"We know she has wings."

Riley cut in. "As much as I hate to say it, I feel I must point out that saving the princess wasn't mentioned in the terms of your agreement. You agreed to find her killer. If there is no killer, your agreement could be null and void. You might not get your father."

Emma's heart sank. Riley was right. If Emma saved the fairy princess, she might end up with nothing. But she wasn't a monster like the fae. She wouldn't sit back and simply let fate play out if she had the chance to stop it. She set her jaw and nodded to herself. "I'll take that risk. If the fairy princess is dead, I'll find her killer. But if she's alive, I'm going to do my best to keep her that way."

"I think you mean *we'll* do our best," Riley said, looking

up from their laptop. "There's no way I'm letting you do this by yourself. Besides, I love ren faires."

"I'm coming too," Sassy said.

"Aren't you supposed to be an impartial judge?" Emma asked.

"Sure. When it comes time to judge, I'll be honest. But that doesn't mean I can't help you solve the case."

Emma smiled. "Glad to have y'all on board. Gresill said this necklace is our ticket to a coronation. He wouldn't have brought it if it wasn't important. Our first step is to figure out when and where this coronation is taking place."

"Easy," Riley said, spinning the laptop around for the others to see. "The Emerald City Ren Faire has an opening ceremony on the first day. The ceremony ends with a coronation of this year's Emerald King or Queen. It's mostly an honorary title, but they get to strut around and pretend to be royalty."

"Sounds like a few people I know," Emma said. "When is the coronation scheduled?"

"The faire opened today, so the opening ceremony will happen this evening. They're opening a time capsule, which buys us a little time, so the coronation"—Riley glanced at the wall clock—"should take place in around three hours. It's just enough time to get there if we leave now."

"Then what are we waiting for?" Emma said. "Let's roll."

CHAPTER 9
VIP

E mma," Sassy said, his tone low and dangerous. "Would you please ask Riley not to hit every pothole this side of the shadow realm? Some of us don't have seat belts, and I'm getting a little tired of catching air."

"I will not," Emma replied. Traffic had added an hour to their trip, and her butt was numb from sitting in the car for so long. She shifted in her seat and struggled to hide the annoyance in her voice. "You're not the only one who's ready to stretch their legs. But in case you haven't noticed, we're driving in a literal field."

It might have been a grassy field in the offseason, but the ren faire had transformed it into an enormous parking lot. Rows of parked cars, SUVs, and trucks were arranged into a maze which smelled more like gasoline than grass. Ahead, a man wearing a safety-orange vest over a court jester's outfit waved a neon-pink baton. Riley turned down the aisle, and the path grew even bumpier.

"I forgot about the parking situation," Riley said, gripping the wheel tightly with both hands. "It's always a mess, but I don't usually drive."

"You've been here before?" Emma said.

"I try to make it every year, though I skip the opening ceremonies. Too many people. In fact, I planned to attend tomorrow with Marcus and a few other folks from the community theater." Riley pulled into an open spot, shifted to park, and cut the engine. "You wouldn't believe the costume Marcus made."

"Excuse me? Marcus? Dressing up?" Emma tried to bend her mind around the idea that serious, careful Marcus would dress up for a ren faire.

"Yeah, he 3D printed a whole suit of armor, then painted it to look like real metal. You should ask him to show you sometime. It's amazing." Riley looked down and bit their bottom lip. "It's a shame we didn't have time to make costumes."

"Is it?" To Emma, it felt like more of a relief than a shame.

"You don't understand. We're not just visiting the ren faire to have fun. We're coming to find Isolde, the fairy. We can't do that without the help of the locals."

"The locals?"

"The performers, the vendors, the people who eat and breathe ren faires even during the offseason. We need them to take us seriously, but if we show up dressed like tourists, they won't give us the time of day."

"You can't be serious. You're telling me that these *locals* won't even talk to us if we're wearing normal clothes?"

"The entire reason that they go to ren faires is to get away from the real world. They can't exactly stop people from wearing modern clothes, but they can avoid them."

"Can we buy costumes?" Emma groaned inwardly. She could already feel the money she'd earned earlier that day slipping through her fingers. She unlatched her seat belt and let it whir back into its mechanism.

"Maybe." Riley's brow furrowed in concentration, then a broad grin spread across their face. "But then again, we may not need to. Let me check in the back of the car."

"For what?" Emma asked, but Riley had already opened their door, jumped out, and popped the back hatch.

Emma opened her door and looked at the ground. If it had once been a beautiful field, it was on its way to becoming a muddy mess, rutted from all the cars coming and going. She stood and stretched and rolled her neck from side to side, working out the kinks. She took a grateful breath of the cool air and looked around. The sun was low, but there was still light enough to see. She heard the faint sounds of a flute. In the distance, a pointy castle turret rose above the dark forest canopy. Sassy jumped out of the car and landed at Emma's feet. They walked around back, where Riley had taken the lid off a large blue plastic tub and was digging through its contents.

"Why does it not surprise me that you have a wardrobe full of costumes in the back of your car?" Emma said.

"They're hand-me-downs," Riley said, still digging. "I talked with a theater professor at the university and mentioned the community theater didn't have many costumes. He was getting rid of some, so I took them off his hands. I stuck them in the back of my car and then forgot them there for six months."

"What kind of costumes?" Emma craned her neck to look over Riley's shoulder, but all she saw was a flash of green velvet.

"A full set of costumes for one of the most iconic plays of all time."

"Spill it." Emma already knew she wouldn't like the answer.

"Peter Pan!" Riley beamed, holding up a green felt jacket.

Emma blinked. "I don't care how many fairies get killed. I'm not dressing up like Peter Pan."

"Of course not. I will play the titular role."

"Who am I, then? Wendy?"

"Even better!" Riley reached into the box and produced a

black tricorn hat with white piping. On its front was stitched a little skull and crossbones. "I was thinking Captain Hook." Riley handed her the hat, which was followed by a long floppy pair of boots and a crimson velvet waistcoat.

"No hook?"

Riley shook their head. "Unfortunately, no. But we are in luck. Due to some… bold casting choices by the university theater, we even have a costume for Sassy."

"I would rather die," Sassy's outraged voice called up.

"He's thrilled," Emma translated.

At first Emma couldn't make heads or tails of the costume Riley held up. It was a bright red, cat-sized vest, and from it dangled hundreds of small yellow, blue, and green fabric triangles.

"Sassy gets to be Captain Hook's parrot!" Riley said.

"Over my dead body," Sassy said.

Emma would have said something, but she was doubled over laughing. Just the thought of the captain of the Night Watch in a parrot costume made her convulse in crying, snorting laughter.

"It's not funny," Sassy said.

"It is though!" Emma squealed, then broke out in fresh laughter. With some effort, she forced herself to take a long, wheezing breath. "Okay. All right. I'm fine. I'm not going to— I'm not even going to think about laughing. This is very serious business."

"It doesn't feel that way to me," Sassy said.

"Look, I don't want to wear a costume either. But Riley's right. We need the locals to help us if we ever hope to find Isolde. It'll be ten times harder if we look like outsiders."

"Blast it, Emma. They're costumes from a play! No one will ever think they're historically accurate."

"And you think that dragons are historically accurate?" Emma pointed at a half-dragon-half-sport-utility vehicle rolling down the aisle, looking for a parking spot.

"I won't do it. I have my pride."

"Look, Sassy, you said it yourself that this place is going to be swarming with paranormals. You can't tell me that in all your years with the Watch, you haven't run afoul of any of them? That you've never been so determined to root out the fae that you leaned on somebody a little too hard? That you've never made any enemies? What if one of them recognizes you?"

Sassy looked like he'd just bitten into something rotten. "It'd make it a hell of a job to complete the investigation. I'll… do it, but promise me you won't take any pictures. If any of this gets back to the Watch, I swear I'll—"

"There's no need to swear." Emma took the parrot costume. "Now let's get you dressed so we can go save the princess… if she's not already dead."

"Whatever we do, we'd better do it fast," Riley said. "There's a heck of a line."

———

It was growing dark when they neared the front of the line. Fairy lights hung from trees clicked on and supplemented the meager sunlight. The mouth-watering scents of roasting turkey legs, funnel cakes, and caramel corn hung in the crisp autumn air. The cool had been a welcome relief from the car's stuffiness, but now it was almost chilly. The sun-and-moon charm, which she wore around her neck, felt cold on her sternum. Emma was glad she had the red pirate overcoat. She hugged it tighter around her.

"Will you be still?" Sassy said from his perch on her shoulder. "I'm having a devil of a time holding on as it is."

That was the other good thing about the overcoat. It gave Sassy someplace to sink his sharp claws. "You could always walk beside me."

"And blow our cover? I never heard of a parrot walking on four legs."

They'd been over this before. She'd told Sassy every which way that he wasn't *actually* trying to fool anyone into thinking he was a parrot. After all, who ever heard of a parrot with whiskers? But the only way he seemed to be able to reconcile the bird suit with his feline dignity was to take it all way too seriously and act like he was deep undercover. Emma slipped a finger under her collar and scratched her neck where the costume made it itch. Sassy wobbled but didn't complain.

Riley vibrated with happy energy. The bright green Peter Pan costume fit them like a glove, and honestly, it worked. Riley looked like they were born to play Peter Pan. In any case, their costume didn't seem to itch anything like Emma's.

From the parking lot, the castle turret seemed far away, deep in the woods. Up close, Emma saw it marked the entry to the faire. At its base was a kind of box office, like at a movie theater, only larger and rounder and infinitely more rustic.

"Next!" one of the cashiers called in a nasal, east-coast voice. She was in her early twenties and dressed like Guinevere or Maid Marian. She wore a tall powder-blue cone-shaped hat with tulle erupting from the top and cascading down her back.

"Two tickets please," Riley said.

"Is that a… cat?" She didn't do a very good job hiding her laugh. "Craziest thing I seen all day, and boy, do they make them crazy around here. But I've got some good news for you. Only humans need to buy tickets, hon. Service animals get in free." She looked over her shoulder, then continued in hushed tones. "The boss would try to charge for animals if they could get away with it, but the law's the law."

Riley looked confused. "The two tickets were for two humans, myself and Captain Hook."

"Captain Hook don't need a ticket, sweetie. Not with that VIP pass around his—ah, her—neck."

"In that case, I'll take one ticket."

"That'll be thirty-five dollars. Cash or charge?"

"Cash," Emma cut in. She pulled her wallet from her breast pocket, handed the cashier a hundred-dollar bill.

"Do you want your change in emerald tokens? They're like money for games and food and things. They don't take cash inside. Something about it messing with the ambiance." Her voice lowered to a conspiratorial tone again. "If you ask me, it's all a scam to get more money. But either way, you've got to have them."

"Sure, I'll take the tokens," Emma said. She was surprised when the cashier handed her thirteen small, octagonal copper coins stamped with the outline of an emerald. "Shouldn't there be more?"

"Five bucks a token. What did I tell you? It's a total rip-off," the cashier said, looking past them to the head of the line. "Next!"

Emma opened her wallet, unzipped the coin holder, and dropped her thirteen emerald tokens in with the priceless Roman coin. "I had no idea ren faires were so expensive."

"Welcome to geekdom," Riley said. "Childlike joy at grownup prices."

Emma followed Riley in a daze through the gate, down a dark cobblestone footpath lined with ash trees until they arrived in a large clearing the size of a village square. The air was filled with music. The space overflowed with people dressed as knights, princesses, and jesters. Interspersed with them were people in fantastical costumes. Half-man-half-horse centaurs trotted by. A group of three red devils sloshed tankards of a fizzy brown liquid. There were angels and demons and wood nymphs but, so far, no fairies.

Suddenly the crowds parted. Two men dressed in leather armor and linen tunics raised long trumpetlike instruments to their lips and blew a shrill, metallic fanfare. They lowered their instruments, and the larger man cleared his throat. "Hark and hear ye! Commenceth now, in the Palladian Amphitheater, the coronation of Ezell Fairykin as Emerald Queen! Glory to her name!"

"Glory to her name!" the crowd replied in unison. Then the band kicked into a jolly, rollicking tune, and all hell broke loose.

CHAPTER 10

GRIFFIN

The crowd of costumed fairgoers pressed Emma on all sides. It moved forward like a flood, slow and relentless. Sassy, still undercover as Captain Hook's parrot, perched on her shoulder, hanging on to her red woolen coat with his claws. He was heavy and Emma's shoulder ached, but the weight reassured her. Thank goodness Sassy was tethered to her. Riley had disappeared into the sea of people.

A Minotaur's coarse brown fur pressed against Emma's arm. His breath steamed in the cool evening air, and he smelled like a barnyard. She side-eyed him. Was this a man in a costume, or could this be one of the paranormals Sassy said were drawn to the faire?

It was easy to pick out the locals, the people who lived for the ren faire. They were the folks wearing handsewn tunics made with handwoven cloth. They were the women with hair braided in elaborate Celtic knots and the men carrying elaborate reproduction broadswords, katanas, or rapiers. But here and there throughout the crowd were people who had opted for less conventional costumes, or perhaps they had come as they were.

Just ahead, a short man wearing green face paint and

tights carried a polished wooden club. He leaned over and spoke to a woman with short brunette hair and a long red tail. Immediately to their right, a tall teenage boy wearing pointy elven ears held his phone up over the crowd, recording a video. He shouted a narration, but Emma couldn't make out the words over the crowd. Emma shuddered. How could she know who was human and who was something else? What had she gotten herself into?

"Did you hear that announcement?" Sassy said into her ear.

"How could I have missed it?" Emma replied, tugging at her collar. Her red wool coat had been a blessing against the cool breeze earlier, but here, in the press of people, it felt swampy. Emma forced herself to focus. Her first step was to find Riley. Emma scanned the crowd for her friend, but the mass of people was too dense, and it was getting dark.

"Ezell Fairykin," Sassy said. "Does the name ring any bells? She's about to be crowned Emerald Queen."

"No." Emma craned her neck, looking for the white feather on top of Riley's Peter Pan hat. This was just her luck. They'd been inside the gates for a total of ten minutes. They were late to the coronation, Riley was missing, and there were so many people she couldn't breathe. Emma felt a sharp prick on her shoulder. "I don't know anybody named Ezell— Ouch!" Emma scowled at Sassy, who had sunk his claws through the coat and into her shoulder. "What the heck?"

"Ezell Fairykin. Think!"

"It'd be a lot easier to think if you weren't stabbing me! I told you, I don't know any—" Emma froze. Suddenly she saw it, the connection that Sassy was hinting at. But the thought was so new, so fleeting, that any sudden movement could send it flying, never to be seen again. Emma began speaking slowly, working her way through the puzzle, feeling the weight of each word on her tongue. "If I was a fairy princess slumming in the human world, I might not want anyone to know that I was a fairy princess."

"It took you long enough."

Emma's heart beat faster as the thought gained momentum. Words tumbled out of her. "I would want to blend in with the humans. First, I'd need a more modern name. You don't see many Isoldes these days. But if I picked something too different from my real name, I might not react to it naturally. So I need an alias that sounds like my real name. Isolde becomes Ezell. And the last name: Fairykin. It's just like something a fairy-obsessed human would call herself." Sure, it sounded fake, but that was the point. Everyone would assume she had made it up, and they wouldn't ask too many questions, especially not at a ren faire. Emma felt an electric shock run up her spine. "If Isolde is really Ezell, then she's still alive!"

"But not for long. Gresill said her doom has a deadline: midnight tonight." Sassy stretched his neck and examined the crowd. "One thing's clear. We won't be able to do anything unless we exit this stampede. I'll cut us a path." Sassy lifted his right paw and unsheathed five razor-sharp claws. He swiped them at the tall teenager, who yelped and rubbed his elf ear.

"What are you doing?" Emma whispered. "You can't just go around scratching people!"

"Are you going to argue ethics with me, or are you going to move?"

Sure enough, the scratch he gave the teen had stunned him, opening an Emma-sized hole in the crowd just in front of him. Emma merged into it. She still couldn't see Riley or much of anything beyond the people boxing her in. "Do you have a plan? Or are you making this up as you go?"

"O, ye of little faith." Sassy raised his paw again and swiped a blond, middle-aged woman with her face painted like a dragon. She looked around incredulously but didn't seem to notice the cat in the parrot costume. Maybe Sassy's commitment to being deep undercover was paying off. While searching for the source of the scratch, the woman slowed, and Emma moved right again.

Sassy lifted his paw one more time, ready to swipe at a person in a green tunic with a green cap and white feather sticking out.

"Stop!" Emma shouted. "That's Riley!"

Riley turned, their face blank with confusion, then their gray eyes locked on Emma's and they let out a breath. "I thought I lost you. The page announced the coronation, then everyone and their sister rushed toward the royal court. I knew the house of Fairykin was popular, but this is bananas."

"We have to reach Ezell," Emma said. "We think that she's really Isolde, the fairy princess. We have to find her and warn her." But as soon as she heard her own words, Emma's heart sank. How could they possibly reach Ezell before the coronation? They were trapped in the middle of an enormous crowd. Even if Sassy scratched everybody, they'd never reach the front of the crowd before the coronation began. Heck, they'd be lucky to reach it before the faire shut down for the night.

Riley frowned and pushed their large round glasses farther up their nose. "I might have a solution to our problem. This isn't the only path to the royal court."

Emma looked left and right. It was hard to see past the crowd, but here and there she caught glimpses of tall plywood barricades painted gray and black to imitate stone walls. "It doesn't look like there's another path. They have us penned in pretty good."

"Yeah, but did you ever stop to think what's behind those barricades? I volunteered a couple of years ago. There were two paths. One for the public and one for staff and emergency services."

"I think stopping a murder counts as an emergency service," Emma said.

"Me too." Riley looked to their right. "If we make it to one of the barricades, we should be able to find a way through."

"Say no more," Sassy replied. He unsheathed his claws and went to work.

———

A few minutes later, they were standing on the opposite side of the barricade. It was cool here and quieter, and it smelled like pine from the unpainted two-by-four scaffolding that braced the large wooden panels against the crowd on the other side. Emma felt the tension drain from her shoulders as she got used to having personal space again. She stretched her neck from side to side and looked around.

She had expected the space beyond the barricade would be like the shoulder of a highway, dirty and cramped. Instead, they stood on a two-lane asphalt road. Temporary streetlamps powered by humming generators bathed the road in an eerie sodium light contrasting with the dark forest beyond.

"It looks like this is a straight shot to the royal court," Riley said. "There's a kind of backstage area where the officials will probably be waiting before the coronation. If we're quick enough, we can make it before the coronation."

Some people were built for running. No matter how early in the morning Emma staggered bleary-eyed from her bed, she could always look out her window onto Undertown Square and see some dedicated soul jogging along the footpaths. Sometimes she would take her coffee and stagger out to her front porch to enjoy the air. Inevitably, the runners would wave and smile. She was sure that they were decent, normal people. But she knew deep down that she would never truly understand them. She would never be a runner.

Still, there were times when running seemed a regrettable yet necessary course of action. This was one of them. She used her right hand to hold Sassy tight against her shoulder. "Let's do this," Emma said.

"And just where do you think you're going?" an unfamiliar voice said from behind them.

Emma choked on her breath, and her stomach did a somersault. She set her jaw and turned to see a short, rotund man strutting toward them. He was in his midfifties with olive skin and curly hair. A watch chain hung from his double-breasted suit. He wore a top hat and carried a walking stick. The effect was more robber baron than ren faire, and it brought Emma up short. "I—"

"To the court." Riley cut in. "The sheriff told us they need reinforcements. A heck of a crowd this year."

"So you're volunteers? Funny, I don't remember seeing you at the orientation." His voice had a clipped, businesslike tone. Even though he was a head shorter than Emma, he seemed to look down at them. "Where are your badges?"

"Lost."

"That's a serious matter."

"Have you seen the crowd out there?" Riley's voice rose. "It's twice as big as last year, and they're animals! Once the page announced the coronation, everybody went crazy and we were pushed in with the crowd. They saw our badges and lanyards and ripped them off us! Whoever set up the faire this year really underestimated the crowd size. We could have gotten hurt!"

The man paused for a moment and seemed pensive. "It's the Fairykins. They've thrown a wrench into everything this year by swarming in and voting Ezell as queen. Not to mention the blasted time capsule. Everyone just can't wait to find out what grizzled and unfathomable relics will be unearthed from the distant past."

"How distant?" Emma couldn't help but ask.

"Nineteen ninety-six."

"Great, now I feel like a grizzled relic."

"Although they're likely to walk away disappointed." A cloud passed across his face, then he suddenly grinned. "However, ticket sales are through the roof, so that's a silver lining."

"Or a golden one," Emma said.

"Indeed." The man looked hard at them, then seemed to reach some conclusion. He produced two large yellow cards attached to neon-pink cords from his jacket pocket and offered them to Riley and Emma. "I'll forgive the loss of your badges this time. Do it again and you're off the team. Here are two temporary badges that will let you access the staff areas. You can return these tomorrow to the comptroller at the main entrance."

"Will do," Emma said, taking her badge and hanging it around her neck.

"This path will take you straight to the court. Be sure to go straight to the court. Stay away from the work crew at the world tree. They've run into a bit of… trouble." He turned on his heel and walked a few steps, then stopped and looked over his shoulder. "And tomorrow when you show up, do me a favor and leave the parrot at home." Without waiting for a reply, he walked back in the direction he'd come, his walking stick tapping rhythmically on the asphalt.

"Squawk!" Sassy said, smirking.

Emma watched the man until he was out of earshot, then turned to Riley. "Who was that? Daddy Warbucks?"

"Richard Griffin. He owns the ren faire."

"It's not a volunteer thing?"

"It's very much a volunteer thing, but Mr. Griffin owns it," Riley said, as if it made perfect sense.

A cool breeze blew down the causeway. Emma shivered.

She'd thought the ren faire would be a bunch of nerds in a public park, but it turned out things were more complicated than she ever could have imagined. Far ahead, trumpets sounded a fanfare, and a cheer went up from the crowd. "It sounds like it's starting! We're too late!"

CHAPTER 11
UNDERCOVER

Emma ran toward the sound of trumpets. The barricade walls, nothing more than sheets of plywood raised on their edges and held in place by a crude lumber framework, wobbled as the crowd on the other side tried to go faster. It was eerie being so close to such a large crowd but not being part of it. To move freely when, just a moment ago, she'd been pinned in. But she wasn't a runner. Riley was already far ahead.

Emma's heavy red overcoat didn't help. It billowed behind her like a cape. The breeze helped dissipate some of the heat from the sudden exercise but not enough to stop beads of sweat from rolling down her back. Sassy clung to her shoulder, doing his best to look like a parrot.

"Do you think you could try to be a little more graceful?" he said. "I thought those potholes in the parking lot were jarring."

"If you don't like it," Emma replied, panting, "why don't you get down and run yourself?"

"Parrots don't run."

"It's not like you're fooling anyone with your parrot act."

"I fooled Griffin."

"He must be half-blind."

"It's called being deep undercover. It's a state of mind."

"Fine, be a parrot. But I'm not feeding you any crackers." Emma caught up to Riley, who was speaking with a tall guard in front of a forged iron gate. Beyond it, in what must have been the royal court, the crowd all spoke at once and sounded like waves crashing on the beach. She tilted her head and looked through the iron bars, but all she saw were the people immediately in front of the gate.

"I don't care if you are volunteers," the guard told Riley. He wore thick glasses on an acne-pocked nose and a full suit of chain mail. "If you don't have a coronation ticket, you don't get in."

"But Mr. Griffin said—"

"Mr. Griffin knows the rules. If he wanted you to attend the coronation, he would have given you a ticket." He took off his glasses and polished them with a small microfiber cloth. He slid them onto his nose and sighed. "Hey, I get it. You worked all day and wanted to see the big event. Any other year, I'd be happy to look the other way and let you in. But this year is totally crazy. The court's packed. There's barely room for all the people with actual, you know, tickets."

Tickets? Emma suddenly became aware of the cold metallic circle resting on her sternum. She touched it. Hadn't Gresill said the sun-and-moon charm would get them into the coronation? She pinched the charm between her fingers and held it out for the guard to see. "What about this?"

"What about what? Oh… Wow. Where did you get that?"

"An… acquaintance gave it to me." She sure wouldn't call Gresill a friend. "He said it was my ticket. It's a VIP pass."

"I know what it is." The guard bit his lower lip and hesitated. "It's not just a VIP pass, it's a founder pass. When they started the faire in the eighties, they forged eight passes, one for each of the founders. They wanted to make sure that no matter how much time passed or how far apart they grew, each of the founders would always command a place of honor at the faire. They reenact the forging every year at the opening except this year because of that silly time capsule. Are you… one of the founders?"

"I… have the founder pass, don't I? And I demand entrance to the coronation!"

"This is above my pay grade. I'll have to ask." He turned and looked past the gate, apparently seeking someone who could take Emma and her place of honor off his hands. Suddenly a series of shrill whistles pierced the air. The guard listened intently, then relaxed. "I'm sorry, but that's the signal."

"For what?"

"Maximum capacity. We can't legally allow anyone else into the royal court. If we do, the fire marshal could shut down the whole faire. Maybe come a little earlier next time? Or, you know, buy a normal ticket."

"Thanks for the advice," Emma said, but the guard had already slipped through the gate and was locking it behind him. She glared at him and sighed. "Riley?"

"Yeah?"

"Why does everything have to be so hard?"

"Well"—Riley stroked their chin—"that depends on who you ask. Different cultures have different explanations. There is, of course, the biblical story about the snake and the apple. Though most scholars would argue that our modern conception of *original sin* deviates from a strict interpretation of the primary—"

"Riley?"

"Um… yeah?"

"I didn't really want an answer."

"You didn't." Riley squinted. "Then why did you ask?"

"Because I want to figure out how to get past this stupid gate to reach Ezell in time and warn her. Hey, didn't you say that this path would take us to a kind of backstage area?"

"Yeah," Riley said, glancing farther down the path. "This used to be it. They must have changed the layout from the last time I was here. The path dead-ends ahead. There are the other gates, of course, but they lead to other parts of the faire. None of them would take us backstage."

"So really, we're not any closer than we were before." It was all too much: the weight of her responsibility, the weight of this stupid wool coat, the weight of Sassy on her shoulder. Emma leaned on the gate and allowed herself to sink slowly to the ground.

Beyond the gate, the crowd suddenly hushed, and an amplified voice rang out. "In the name of our founders, welcome, one and all, noble and commoner, human and… other, to the forty-third coronation of the Emerald City Ren Faire!"

A jolt of electricity ran through Emma's body. This was no time for moping. She had to do something, and she had an idea. "Sassy?"

"Present."

"Can fairies talk to cats?"

"I'm not a cat, I'm a parrot."

"Just… stop method acting and answer me! Can fairies understand cats?"

"Well, I never met a fairy, so I wouldn't know. But the fae can speak with cats. It's part of that treaty Gresill went on about. If the fairies are related to the fae… maybe? What are you driving at?"

"Riley and I can't get through that gate, but the bars are wide enough for you to slip through. You'll be able to move through the crowd too. I want you to go ahead, find Ezell or Isolde or whatever her name is, and warn her. Maybe Gresill thinks this murder is a foregone conclusion, but we have to stop it if we can."

"That would be a brilliant plan if I was a cat."

"Will you please give up the parrot act?"

"What act? I'm a parrot." He looked at her defiantly. "Squawk!"

Emma's vision narrowed to a tight circle filled with red. "Fine. Fine. I'm sorry. You are… obviously a parrot, but if there's the slightest chance that this fairy might be able to speak with… parrots, then you could still warn her."

Sassy was silent for a moment, apparently weighing his decision. "I'll do it. I'll be a hero. Not for myself, but for all parrotkind."

"Wonderful!" Emma couldn't hide the sarcasm dripping from her voice. "Now fly!"

Sassy, finally, left Emma's shoulder. What a relief it was to have that weight off her. She stood and rolled her right shoulder, then her neck, and winced at how stiff she was. When she looked to her right, Sassy was already gone, slipped through the gate. What would the people in that crowd think when they looked down and saw a cat in a parrot costume threading through their legs?

"Mostly," Riley said. "I don't envy you. Talking to spirits seems to be a lot of work. Connecting to everything that ever lived seems, well, overwhelming. But I really, really wish I could have heard the other side of that conversation just now."

"I really, really wish I hadn't heard it." Emma reached around back and dusted off the long coat where she had sat. She turned around. "Did I ruin it?"

Riley looked the coat up and down. "Nothing that a stain stick won't get out. But more importantly, what do we do now?"

Emma frowned. "We can't just wait around for Sassy to save the day. He might be delayed, or he might not be able to communicate with Ezell, or she might decide that a cat in a parrot costume is fundamentally untrustworthy. No, we have to keep trying. If this path doesn't take us backstage, then some other path will. We just need to loop around and find it."

Riley shook their head. "I don't know my way around as well as I thought I did. Where would we even start?"

"Whoa, man, is that Emma and Riley?" a voice called from behind them.

Emma turned to see a man with shaggy blond hair and a neatly trimmed beard. He wore a single-piece undyed linen robe, tied at the waist with a strand of rope that looked like it had been hand-spun from locally foraged grasses. Around his neck he wore half a dozen necklaces filled with white quartz, red agate, and purple amethyst. He was carrying a large, clear plastic tub filled with similar necklaces. "Orion? What are you doing here?"

"Are you kidding? I always work the ren faires, man. It's a fun time. I just close the crystal shop down, dress up like a wizard, set up a tent, and wait for the moolah to roll in. Plus I get to hang outside, eat good food— Hey, have you tried one of those giant smoked turkey legs yet? They're just... chef's kiss, man."

"Chef's kiss?"

"Yeah, like the best."

"But you don't say 'chef's kiss.'"

"Sure you do! It's like, the best. Just... chef's kiss."

"No." Emma shook her head. "It's a gesture. You put your fingertips together by your mouth and make a kissing sound."

"Emma's right," Riley added.

"Whatever, man. I didn't call the grammar police."

"It's not grammar— You know what? Never mind. Are you going to the coronation? We're dying to get in." Emma decided not to mention the details about why they wanted to go. She didn't know how he would take the news about the fairy. With most people, she would have to worry that they wouldn't believe her. But with Orion, it was the opposite.

He'd believe her too much. After all, the last time she'd seen him, he'd been convinced that vampires were out to get him.

"The coronation, huh? Everybody seems to want to go. I always skip it. It's a real snooze fest. Hey, why don't you guys come back to my tent? I just made a fresh pot of peppermint tea. I haven't seen you around the courtyard shops much. A lot of good changes are happening."

"Maybe another time?" Emma said. "We're really anxious to see the coronation. They… have a time capsule this year. It seems superinteresting."

"Incredibly interesting," Riley added, somewhat unconvincingly.

"All right. Well, I've got to go restock this merchandise. Nessa's in charge of the shop, and she's not very good at working the cash register. You should stop by later."

"Definitely," Emma said. "Right after we sneak into the coronation."

"Forgot to buy your ticket, huh? The fortune teller in the stall next to mine said he was going to slip in too. He said there's a hole in the fence on the north side of the world tree. Takes you right next to the stage." Orion turned to leave. "Well, it's been a blast, but I'm going to skedaddle."

Emma turned to Riley. "Do you know where the world tree is?"

"Yeah. Everything else might have changed, but it's not like you can move a tree." Riley paused. "But didn't Mr. Griffin tell us to stay away from the world tree?"

Emma squinted and tried to remember the conversation. "His exact words were to stay away from the work crew by the world tree. If what Orion says is true, we shouldn't have any problem doing that. We'll just walk around them, find the hole in the north side of the gate, and slip through without anyone ever knowing we're there."

"Famous last words."

CHAPTER 12
GONE

"Why do they call it the world tree anyway?"

"World tree legends are present in several cultures, though the Norse mythologies are the most familiar to people. The idea is that the world tree connects the heavens above to the normal terrestrial world, then down to the underworld through the roots."

"And this tree does all that?"

"No." Riley laughed. "It's just a normal maple tree in a field, but they needed to call the field something, so they called it the field of the world tree. It's just over this way." Riley led Emma to another gate, which opened into a big grassy field. In the fading evening light, the field looked dark and mysterious except for a spot in the center where a work crew had set up three of the portable streetlights in front of a maple tree.

"That's it?"

"Not what you were expecting?"

"I thought it'd be bigger, I guess." Emma peered at the work crew, trying to make out what they were doing. The crew was made up of three men. Two of them wore the rags of medieval peasants. They carried shovels, and their faces were covered in dirt. The third man's face was clean. He wore white breeches and a red shirt. He stood at the edge of a large pit and stared in. As he stroked his chin, Emma got the impression that he was a man who didn't know what to do.

Suddenly the man looked up and saw them. He motioned them over with his hand. "You there! Come help us!"

Emma froze. Just what she needed. Another distraction. She waved at the man. "It's okay! We're busy!" Then she whispered to Riley. "Hurry up. Let's get out of here."

"I say!" The man in the red shirt shouted. "You wear the sigil of the Saturday Afternoon Volunteer Crew! Come and lend your hand to our most important task!"

"No, thanks! We're good!" Emma called over her shoulder on the way to the north wall. When Orion had told them to look for the loose section, it seemed so simple. But she hadn't known then just how freaking big the wall would be. She hadn't known either that it wouldn't be a plywood wall like the others earlier but an actual stone-and-mortar construction.

"As assistant deputy warden, I'm afraid I must insist that you join your labor to our own. If you shirk once more your duties, I will be forced to report you to the first deputy warden. Your badges will be stripped as will your titles. Your ancestral lands will be confiscated and your people driven in chains away from hearth and home."

Emma leaned to Riley and whispered, "Why is he talking like that?"

"It's a ren faire thing," Riley replied. "Some people really get into the fancy accents. They're usually pretty bad at it though."

The warden seemed not to hear them. "If you join your strength to ours, your name will forever be known in the kingdom. Long from now, when bards sing songs of the raising of the 1996 time capsule, your brave deeds will be remembered. What sayest you?"

Emma looked back at the wall, and her heart sank. She

hoped Sassy was having better luck warning Ezell, because Emma was never going to make it in time. She inspected the man approaching her. He was about her height. Close up, she saw that his red shirt was made from velvet. Even in the cool evening air, it must have been boiling hot. She turned to Riley. "Do we have a choice?"

"I don't think so. After all, he is the assistant deputy warden."

"It doesn't sound that impressive," Emma replied.

"Really, guys," the warden said, breaking character and talking in a New Jersey accent. "We just need some help opening the time capsule. It will only take a minute. We already dug the hole, but the fricking time capsule is too much for a couple of people."

Emma squinted against the bright work lights and waited for her stinging eyes to adjust. The pit was deeper than she'd thought at first, a full six feet. At the bottom of it sat a large, unadorned concrete box. It was stained a reddish brown from the dirt.

It didn't look like a time capsule.

Emma had seen one unearthed in elementary school. It had been a short section of thick PVC pipe, capped on the ends. Later, when she was living in Tulsa, the local chamber of commerce opened another time capsule from the sixties. It had been a steel box around the size of a laundry basket. But the box at the bottom of the pit must have been at least six feet long and three feet wide.

It was probably a mistake, but Emma felt drawn to the time capsule. Questions swirled around her brain. Why had they made it so large? What was inside? Would it still be intact? Or would water have soaked through the porous concrete and reduced the contents to a moldy sludge?

The warden must have picked up on her hesitation. "Nobody knew the thing would be this big. We all thought maybe it would be the size of a shoebox. We expected to come out here, dig it up, and take it to the royal court where the Emerald Queen could open it up in front of the crowd. All that went out the window when we hit this freaking gigantic concrete box. Now we have a new plan. Open it here, take the stuff out, and transport it to the court."

"That's not going to be very dramatic," Emma said.

"We're out of options. Even if you two happened to have a magic excavator in your pocket, it wouldn't do any good. The world tree's roots are wrapped around the box's base. We can't pull it out without damaging the tree. We can't damage the tree without getting in trouble with the planning commission."

Emma stared down at the box. "What's supposed to be in there anyway?"

"Nobody knows exactly, but it's a message from the founders. They buried it here the year that they created the faire."

Emma glanced one last time toward the north wall. In the distance, a cheer went up, punctuated by a big whoosh, then a bang. A green starburst appeared in the sky beyond the wall. It held itself in the air for three heartbeats, then fell. Its green light faded to the color of embers. If they were shooting fireworks and cheering, the coronation must be over. Maybe, just maybe, Sassy had warned Ezell in time to save her.

———

Sassy slipped through the iron bars and into the crowd. When he lost sight of the others, he stopped and shook off that ridiculous parrot costume. He arched his back into a deep, shivering stretch, then shook out his legs and his feet, sore from hanging on to Emma's coat. It hadn't been easy to keep a straight face when pretending to be a parrot. His claws would be numb for the rest of the day. But Emma deserved it for making him wear that humiliating costume in the first place. He'd have to figure out a plausible story for how he'd lost it, but there was plenty of time for that.

He stopped and craned his neck, trying to see which direction would take him to the coronation stage. All he saw was a forest of feet and legs in white and green and black stockings. Unless he was prepared to make an enemy or two, there wasn't any place for him to climb to get a better view. So he made his best guess and set off.

On a quiet day, he might have cocked an ear up to listen for the hollow sound of footsteps on a wooden stage. But the crowd's murmur above and around him drowned out any of those sounds. It wouldn't do any good to wait for the announcer's amplified voice either. Those loudspeakers were placed on poles around the audience.

Scent was equally useless. Though Sassy's nose was the stuff of legend, being so close to that many people with that many feet made him wish his sense of smell wasn't so good. It was almost as bad as that time when headquarters had sent him to Paris to train with the ghost-hunting cats of Notre Dame. He had been tailing his target and took a wrong turn in to a cheese shop. Humans ate the most disgusting things.

It was a sixth sense that he followed now. Was it experience? Intuition? Divinity? He preferred not to call it anything. It was a feeling, shy as any songbird. If you pounced too soon, it'd fly away. But if you took your time, stalked it patiently, and waited for just the right moment? Things usually worked out. That's why he wasn't surprised when he suddenly came upon the coronation stage.

The gray steel barriers were designed to keep humans away from the stage. Sassy had no problem slipping through them and around back into a kind of staging area hidden from the audience.

"Your public grows restless, my queen," a man said. He was dressed like a fool in green-and-purple motley. The toes of his burgundy shoes curled up into circles. On his head, he wore a jester's cap and bells.

"She's not queen until she's crowned," a bearded man wearing brown replied. "And at this rate, I would say that'll happen sometime next year. Until then, she's just Ezell."

"Give it a rest, Brad," a woman in a green chiffon dress said. She had red lips and olive skin and black hair that fell in waves to her bare shoulders. A pair of large wings hung from her back. They looked like nothing so much as dragonfly wings and shone iridescent green in the lamplight. "You know as well as I do that I can't be crowned queen until I pick which crown to wear. Which do you think looks best? The classic gold circlet? Or the woven crown of vines?"

"Classic gold," Brad said. "It's what they've used for all the other coronations. It's classic for a reason."

"That's just the problem, isn't it?" Ezell held one crown in each hand and looked between them. "This isn't just any coronation. I'm the first Emerald Queen from the house of Fairykin. The crown of vines feels more like something a fairy queen would wear. But on the other hand, gold is more expensive."

Sassy's mouth went dry. This had to be Isolde, alias Ezell, the fairy queen doomed to be murdered. He ran to her and leaped onto a barrel next to her. "Hey, fairy, I have a warning for you from Gresill."

Ezell turned toward Sassy. She stared at him, frowning in confusion.

"Hello?" Sassy said. "Earth to fairy. You're in danger."

Her frown spread into a smile, and she leaned over to look at Sassy more closely. "Hello there, cutie. What is your name?"

"It doesn't matter who I am. You have a doom hanging over your head, and the deadline is midnight."

"What a talker you are. And such a big boy."

"Is this a game to you? Don't you understand me? You're in danger!"

"Did you hear him, Brad? I'm very good with animals. It's like he's trying to tell me something. Maybe he wants to pick the crown for me?" She held the two crowns in front of Sassy.

"Don't be a fool, Ezell. We don't have time to pet kitties. If you don't get out on stage and give this crowd a coronation, they're going to have our heads."

Ezell turned and stared daggers at Brad. She sighed and walked toward him. "We'll use the crown of vines. And before we go on, could you help me adjust my wings? The right one's gotten bent again."

"That's because you keep leaning on it," Brad said. He went behind Ezell, grabbed the wing in both hands and tugged. It came off with a click. He spent a moment bending it back into the correct shape, then pushed it into a metal socket protruding from Ezell's dress. The wings weren't real at all. They were a costume…

———

"Let's get this over with." Emma walked to the edge of the pit, almost tripping on a rut in the soil. She looked in. It was deep and wide, with room for several people at the bottom. That made sense, Emma decided, if they had planned to open the time capsule where it rested. A ladder protruded from the pit next to her. She grabbed the top of the ladder and swung her foot onto the top rung.

Emma had hoped her days of climbing into mysterious holes in the ground were over. She'd avoided Undertown's tunnels since her time with the fae. The one time she'd used them she almost had a panic attack, with every smell and sound convincing her that something awful lurked in the shadows. She sent out a silent thanks to whoever brought the construction lights. She reached the bottom. It smelled like humus. She looked up to see Riley and the two workers following her.

"Excellent," the warden called down from the top of the pit. "Use the crow bars to pry the lid up, then you should be able to slide it off and lean it against the edge of the pit."

"You aren't going to help?" Emma shouted up.

"Are you kidding? I'd be a fool to go anywhere near that bog in my white pantaloons. Besides, the role of assistant deputy warden is an administrative position, not that of a common laborer."

"I'm starting to understand why they guillotined all the nobles back in France," Emma shouted.

"If you're going to lead a peasant revolt, do it on your own time! But for now, less talking and more opening."

Emma didn't bother replying. She ran her hand along the top of the box. The concrete felt rough, but traces of dirt felt cool and dry and chalky on her skin. Now that she was inside the pit, she saw that the bottom of the box was, indeed, embedded in tree roots. They wrapped around it like tentacles intent on pulling it deeper into the ground. A black pry bar leaned against the box. She picked it up and tried inserting its thin steel edge in the crack between box and lid. The others did the same.

"Wonderful," the assistant deputy warden called down. "Now on three, everyone lift the lid and push. One… Two… Three!"

Emma pressed her pry bar down, which lifted her section of lid above the box's lip. She waited for the others to do the same, then she pushed. The lid was heavier than she expected, and the loose dirt under her feet felt slippery. She put her right foot against the pit wall and pushed again with everything she had. The lid moved and kept moving! It slid along the top of the box with a deep rumble, then flipped up and thudded onto the ground. Emma bent double and panted.

"What… the hell… is that?" the warden said, looking from above. He jumped onto the ladder and clattered down, streaking his white pantaloons with rust-colored dirt.

Emma glanced up. The open box glowed with eerie greenish light. She stood, looked into the open time capsule, and gasped. There, lying in the center of the open box, was a frail, delicate body. It gave the impression of being made of thin, translucent white paper stretched over a brittle lattice-work of bone. She was dressed in white robes and would have been the most beautiful woman Emma had ever seen, if not for the pair of gossamer fairy wings hugging her shoulders.

"Isolde," Emma whispered. "Is that you? Were we too late?"

Emma felt a cold serpent coil around her heart and squeeze. She winced. She'd been so sure that she and her friends could keep Isolde from being killed. She had convinced herself that when Gresill told them about the coronation, it was because that's when the murder was supposed to take place. When she heard the fireworks and the cheering, she'd let herself believe that Sassy had reached the fairy princess in time. She believed the danger had passed.

She was wrong. Tears welled up in Emma's eyes. She'd felt so clever when she deduced that Ezell was an alias for Isolde, but she'd been wrong. It was nothing more than a coincidence, and now Isolde was dead.

It seemed disrespectful to look straight at the dead fairy princess. But Emma couldn't tear her eyes away. Her face was small and heart-shaped, and her hair was the color of snow. Her eyes were closed. On her red lips sat a small, familiar-looking gold coin.

She reached out half-consciously, retrieved the coin, and examined it. The tail side of the coin depicted a chariot with the word *Roma*. The head side depicted a man in a toga with a laurel wreath. If you ignored a few scuffs and scratches, it exactly matched the priceless coin that Linda had given her. What were the chances of that?

Emma turned to show the coin to Riley, but Riley and everyone else were transfixed on the body in the time capsule. Its eerie green glow became brighter, increasing until it over-powered the halogen flood lamps above. The body glowed like a firefly that didn't know summer was over. It glowed so bright you couldn't see it any more than you could see the looped filament of an incandescent bulb. It glowed so brightly that it created daylight behind Emma's squeezed-shut eyes.

Then suddenly there was a *pop* and a sound like shards of crystal falling. The light went out, and when Emma finally opened her eyes, the body was gone, and the box was empty.

CHAPTER 13
TEA

Emma stood at the bottom of the hole and stared into the empty concrete box. The air was damp and smelled like clay. Above them, the generators hummed and powered the sodium floodlights which lit the people around her, the box, and the world tree's roots in unforgiving blue light.

Riley stood across from her. The two workmen dressed as peasants flanked her on either side. All stared silently, just like Emma did, at the box, each of them coming to their private conclusions about the event they'd witnessed. The assistant deputy warden stood by the ladder. He didn't seem to care that his white trousers were streaked with dirt. His jaw hung open, sweat rolled down his face, and his red velvet shirt trembled as he hyperventilated.

"Are you okay?" Emma asked.

The warden stared unblinking at the open box. It wasn't every day that you saw a dead fairy disappear into a blinding light, but he seemed to be taking it harder than everyone else. Eventually, he looked at Emma, his eyes rimmed with tears. "I can't believe they killed her!"

He was right. Someone had killed Isolde. And now Emma

had to find the killer if she ever hoped to see her father again. A pit opened in her stomach. How was she ever going to solve the case? She had no idea why anyone would want to kill a fairy. She didn't know how she'd been killed. And her Captain Hook costume couldn't hide the fact that she was a complete newcomer to the faire, with no local connections and nowhere to start.

Except that wasn't entirely true. She had the coin, which somehow connected the victim to Linda and the Cappotelli crime family. She had Orion, who was a vendor at the fair and could help her cultivate the relationships she'd need to crack the case. And last, but not least, she had the assistant deputy warden, who just admitted that he knew the victim.

One thing was for certain: they had to get out of that hole. They had to find somewhere safe and quiet to interview the warden. And after all the stress of the past half hour, Emma needed to have a cup of tea. She knew where she could find one.

———

Orion filled a Styrofoam cup with steaming tea from a large thermos flask. Emma took it from him and held it to her lips. Warm steam rose from the hot tea. Emma enjoyed the sensation of it against her face. She breathed in and was filled with the aroma of spearmint. She took a sip and felt the hot liquid travel through her, making her shiver, shaking the tension out of her neck and shoulders.

Closing her eyes, she let herself sink into the plush beanbag chair. The beads inside contoured around her, supporting her, making her feel like she was floating on a cloud.

"Ahem." The sound interrupted Emma's reverie. She opened her eyes and saw Riley looking at her expectantly.

"Sorry," Emma said. She tried to sit upright, but the

beanbag chair fought her. There was a reason, she decided, why nobody had these anymore. Nobody except for Orion.

When he told her that he had set up his crystal shop at the faire, Emma had assumed he'd rented a booth, a couple of folding tables displaying his wares in front of a slick vinyl banner. The reality was much more impressive.

Orion had erected a large, closed tent like desert nomads might use. Intricately patterned crimson-and-white carpets hung from the walls, providing insulation against the crisp fall evening. Tables lined the tent's perimeter, displaying every size and shape and color of the gemstone. The center of the tent had been made into a social space. Half a dozen fur-covered beanbags surrounded a low circular table made of dark polished wood.

"Nice setup you've got here," Emma said.

"Thanks! Nessa did most of it. She's got a knack," Orion said.

"I'm surprised you sell enough crystals to make this setup worth your while. Doesn't look like you get a lot of foot traffic."

"Wholesale, man," Orion said, pouring another cup of tea. "Some faires are all about retail. But this one? Dealers and high-end collectors. People who really know their stuff. The other day a blacksmith came in and bought my whole stock of tsavorite garnet for a commission from the boss himself. Swords or something." Orion poured another cup of tea and handed it to the assistant deputy warden, and then he took the flask to the back of the tent where Vanessa was arranging inventory.

Emma watched the warden as he brought the steaming cup of tea to his lips. They'd had a heck of a time getting him to climb the ladder out of the pit and walk to Orion's tent in the vendor district. He'd been nearly catatonic with fright. The walk had done him good, and he looked almost back to normal except for his thousand-yard stare and a slight tremor in his hands as he held the cup of tea.

"Can you talk?" Emma asked.

"I think so," the warden replied. It was the same New Jersey accent, but the fire was gone. "It was just a heck of a surprise seeing Isolde in that box."

"How did she get there?"

"You think I know? That box was buried six feet deep when me and the guys went out there to dig it up."

"Who told you to dig it up?"

"The boss."

"Griffin?"

"Who else?

"Was the soil disturbed when you arrived?"

"Was it already dug up, you mean? Hard to tell. I wasn't out there to play detective. I was out there to dig a hole. Sure, I was a little surprised at how easy the digging went, but the dirt all around here's basically sand covered in grass."

"Was the grass at the dig site disturbed in any way?"

"There's no grass under the world tree. Never has been."

Emma looked at the ceiling and let out a sigh. She tried to focus on the facts of the case. What, exactly, did she know? She knew Isolde was killed today. She knew they found her buried six feet under in a concrete box. She knew that if the box had any contents previously, they were missing. Could they have been stolen by whoever killed Isolde? Possibly, but it was conjecture, one of infinite facts she didn't yet know. A feeling of despair wormed its way into Emma's heart. How would she ever solve the puzzle with so many missing pieces? How would she ever crack the case when she knew so little about Isolde, about the faire, or possible suspects? Emma pressed her lips together and nodded to herself. There was no use complaining.

Emma faced the warden. "You knew Isolde?"

"Everybody knew her. She was a fixture." He sipped his

tea. "I've been doing the faire for what? Six, seven years? She went back way further than that. Hey, who are you anyway? Why are you asking me questions?"

Emma gestured to the founder pass hanging from her neck. "I've been asked to look into her death by certain entities that wish to remain anonymous."

"One of the founders? I thought they were all dead." He glanced at her skeptically. "So you're a private eye? I never would have guessed it to look at you."

"Let's just imagine that my client was one of the founders. What could you tell me about Isolde?"

"Well, since you're in the know, I guess there's no harm in telling you that it took me a couple of years to realize that she wasn't human. She kept a low profile. Pretended to be one of those girls who dress up like fairies. Some people think they're a new thing, with the Fairykin and all that. Fact is, they've always been around. Made it real easy for Isolde to blend in. Funny how things work. She never went out looking for trouble, but it always found a way to come to her."

Emma leaned in. "What kind of trouble?"

"The faire is like this: there're the normal people, us humans. Then there're the not-humans, whatever you call them. In the real world, the groups don't get together much. But here? The faire? It's like the beach. The ocean meets the land. Isolde lived right on that border. It opened her up to all kinds of abuse. On one hand, you had the Fairykin. They were jealous that she made such a convincing fairy. Didn't know she had the advantage of actually being one. I heard that the new queen— What's her name?"

"Ezell?"

"Yeah, I heard her screaming at Isolde yesterday. Something about a crown being missing? Typical." The warden shrugged. "And then you have her own people. The not-so-human crowd. They gave her a lot of crap about going native.

Truth is, they didn't like the influence she had. Word is a couple of them were trying to squeeze her out of her position."

"What do you mean, her position?"

The warden blinked and glanced at the tent's entrance warily. He looked like someone who had almost walked off a cliff but stopped at the last moment. "I wouldn't know."

"Come on," Emma said. "I'm never going to be able to find her killer if you hold things back. You obviously knew her."

The warden looked at the floor and grimaced. "We talked a couple of times. Mostly, she was just around. I had my job, and she had hers. Am I sad she's dead? Yeah. Do I want the guy to rot in jail? Yeah. But right now I've got something more important to worry about."

"Which is?"

"Saving my own skin." He leaned in and his voice lowered. "If somebody out there didn't hesitate to knock off somebody like Isolde, they wouldn't think twice about coming after a nobody like me."

Emma's blood heated up. This wasn't just about bringing a killer to justice. Her dad's future was at stake. She wanted to grab the warden by his shoulders and shake him until he told the truth. No. She took a deep breath. Violence would just make him clench tighter to the truth. She would have to keep her cool and play the long game. Still, there was one card she hadn't played.

Emma stood, reached into her pocket, and took out the small gold coin that had been on Isolde's lips. She walked over to the warden and held it up for him to see. "This was on Isolde's lips. It was only after I removed it that she started glowing. Do you recognize it?"

The warden stared at the coin, frozen, unblinking. Without seeming to notice, he clenched his hands and crushed his

Styrofoam cup, its pieces falling to the floor like snow. After a long silence, he spoke. "I've never seen a coin like that in my life."

———

"So that guy was definitely lying," Riley said, kicking off their shoes and sitting cross-legged on the beanbag. "Did you see the way he looked at that coin? He was frightened out of his wits!"

Emma sipped her tea. It was her second cup and came from a new batch that Orion had just prepared from fresh mint leaves. Now that the warden had run off, she could take a moment to relax and discuss the case with her friends. "I agree. He was hiding something. I'm not sure I blame him though. Whoever killed Isolde is still out there. They wouldn't think twice about another murder."

"He did let it slip that Isolde has a job that might have gotten her in trouble."

"Yeah, he said the paranormals used her, even though they accused her of spending too much time with humans." Something about that tickled her memory. "Back at my house, Sassy said something that stuck out. He said ren faires are hotspots for smuggling of goods between the human and paranormal worlds. Do you think Isolde might have been involved with that?"

"I couldn't say. I'm still stuck on the problem of the coin. What are the chances of finding the exact same ancient coin twice in one day?"

"Do you think the Cappotellis are involved in this?"

"The evidence is certainly suggestive. It would shed light on one question that I've been pondering. The Cappotelli crime family is based out of Chicago. Why would someone come all the way to Undertown to have a séance?"

Emma puffed up. "Well, I'd like to think I've gained a reputation."

"Yes, a local reputation. It's not something that someone in Chicago would hear about. And even if they did hear about you, why would they choose you over the hundreds of other psychics with reputations?"

"The fae prince did say that my power was unique."

"But how would your client have known that? They can only go by what they hear in the normal human world. The only explanation that makes sense to me is that they were already in Seattle for business. While here, they asked around about a psychic and your name came up."

"And you think that business could be… murder?"

Riley shrugged. "It's been known to happen in that world."

Emma thought back to her session with Linda. It had only been a few hours earlier, but it already seemed like an eternity had passed. Could the self-possessed woman in the navy cardigan be a murderer? Emma didn't want to believe it, though she had to admit that the woman swam in dangerous waters and had managed to survive all these years. "Assuming she was involved in the murder, why leave a coin? If the Cappotellis left the coin with people as a kind of promise to come back, what was the point of leaving it on a corpse? All it does is incriminate her."

"It could be to send a message," Riley suggested.

Emma shook her head. "That doesn't explain the most confusing fact. Isolde only began to disappear after I removed the coin from her lips. It was almost like the coin was holding her there, binding her. Could it contain some magic?"

"I'm stumped," Riley said. "It's common practice in the funerary rites of many cultures to place coins on the closed eyelids of a corpse. I've never heard of placing one on the lips. Unfortunately, I'm not an expert on the magical properties of coins."

"Did somebody say magic coins, man?" Orion looked at them from across the room. "I know just the dude for that."

"Seriously? Here in the faire?" Emma asked. "Who?"

"Merlin. Who else?"

CHAPTER 14
MERLIN

Emma and Riley followed Orion through the maze of shop tents on their way to enlist Merlin's help with the coin. The air was cool and crisp. It smelled like wood smoke and roasting meats. The sun had fully set behind the distant pines, and the only light came from strings of fairy lights crisscrossing above and from the lamps in front of the shops.

Earlier when they'd walked to Orion's, the place had been a ghost town. Now groups of costumed fairgoers began to return from the coronation. They didn't seem disappointed about the empty time capsule. They smiled and laughed, and when a band kicked into a rollicking lyre-and-pipe-and-drum tune, they whooped with joy.

Orion led them past a group of six noblemen lifting broad-bellied tankards in a sloshing toast. They walked past two satyrs linked arm in arm who danced to the music in tight circles, punctuating the drumbeats with little kicks. Orion was in his element. He threaded through the growing crowd and took them into a kind of alleyway, a space behind and between the vendor's stalls.

"Are you sure this is the right way?" Emma asked, stepping over a thick power cable that snaked underfoot.

"Totally," Orion replied. "Merlin's not too big on crowds. It's one of those things where if you know, you know. We're almost there. It's just around the corner."

The situation made less and less sense. Why would someone set up a booth at a festival if they didn't want anyone to find them? And the name Merlin: it had to be fake, right? If she was going to trust this guy, she had to know more about him. "So this friend of yours: why do they call him Merlin?"

Orion shrugged. "Because he's a wizard."

"You mean he dresses up like a wizard for the faire?"

"No, he is one."

"How do you know?"

"Don't ask me, man. I'm not an expert on wizards."

Emma stifled a growl. She'd forgotten how frustrating Orion could be. He would drop a suggestive detail on you like it was the most obvious thing in the world. But if you asked him to elaborate, he turned into the world's most obtuse himbo. With Orion, you could never be sure if you were getting the truth or something he'd convinced himself was the truth.

The smart tactic would have been to wait, meet Merlin, and then make her judgments. But she had a question, and she couldn't help herself. "If you're not an expert on wizards, how do you know that Merlin is one? How do you know wizards even exist?"

"Like, how do I know you exist?" he replied, not turning to see Emma scowl. "Anyway, we're here. You'll see for yourself. But hey, when you go in, don't mention how messy it is. He's real touchy about that."

They stopped in front of a square olive-drab tent, sewn from the same commercial-grade fabric as the others but only slightly larger than Emma's pantry. Merlin's shop didn't have a lamp out front. There was no stream of customers going in and out. It didn't even have a sign. A small line of warm light escaped from under the tent flap.

Orion reached out and pulled the flap open, then gestured to Emma. "Ladies first."

Emma's stomach turned to jelly. With the tent flap open, she should have been able to see inside, but her view was obscured by a patchouli-scented fog that rolled out of the tent and blanketed the ground. It felt strangely warm as it touched her feet and ankles.

From inside the tent came a booming voice, resonant with authority. "Enter!" it said. Emma stepped in.

———

Emma rubbed her eyes and looked around the tent. She'd expected it to be cramped, but it was spacious. Maybe they'd only seen the entrance from where they'd stood in the alley. Inside, the patchouli scent mixed with the bitter odor of turpentine, spicy mint, and a dozen musky, earthy aromas that Emma couldn't name.

Heat radiated from a small cast-iron wood stove in the center of the room. Flames leaped merrily behind the small window into the firebox. Next to the stove, three ancient armchairs sat on threadbare Persian rugs. It was the only open space in the entire tent. The rest was piled from floor to ceiling with all manner of junk.

Plastic milk crates filled with glass doorknobs supported half a dozen wicker baskets full of blue-and-red mushrooms. Huge oil paintings of naked cherubs, Zeus, and Hera leaned in their gilt frames against the tent wall. A five-gallon glass carboy was filled with clear liquid and countless round objects that looked suspiciously like eyeballs. They swiveled and followed Emma as she walked into the room.

Merlin was nowhere to be seen, but from the back of the

tent came a sound like a metal pie pan crashing to the floor. Then the sounds of glass shattering and marbles bouncing. Emma craned her neck to see the source of the noise. She saw item after item being flung up into the air, and then heard them crash on the ground. This was accompanied by a low muttering.

"Where did I put the blasted thing? Could I have filed it under *Aardvarks*? *Armadillos*? No, that would make too much sense. I probably put it somewhere safe. That was my first mistake."

"Hey, Merlin, dude!" Orion called out. "You've got company."

The stream of tossed items stopped, and the tent became silent. "Company? Ahh yes, I remember now. I felt a draft. Did you close the door behind you? I hate the cold."

"It's totally closed."

Emma blinked, and when she opened her eyes, Merlin stood in front of her. If experience had taught her anything, it was that someone named Merlin should look nothing like her conception of Merlin. It was much more likely that he'd be a skinny teenager who knew a lot of yo-yo tricks or a nerdy computer programmer who went to goth clubs on the weekend. But the Merlin who stood in front of her now was the exception that proved the rule.

If you called up central casting and asked for a rumpled old wizard with a gray felt hat, a long white beard, and a slightly insane glint in his eye, you couldn't have gotten a better match. The only thing about Merlin that wasn't quite wizardly were the scarves. Over his standard-issue wizarding robes, he wore a two-inch-thick stack of chunky woolen scarves.

Emma stepped forward. "Excuse us for intruding, but Orion was just telling me that you might be able to help us with the matter of—"

"Silence!" the wizard boomed. He lifted his nose and

breathed in deeply, then sniffed several times in short succession and frowned. He reached a bony finger out toward Emma. "This one smells of the dead. Orion, why have you brought this here?"

"Well, ah." Orion rubbed the back of his neck.

"Excuse me," Emma interrupted. "This one has a name."

Merlin frowned, then spoke in the tone of a lecturer in some very dusty and very boring subject. "To be grammatically correct, you should say that you had a name."

"Orion, what have you gotten me into? This man is crazy."

The wizard continued without seeming to notice what she said. "To say that you have a name implies that you are still living. But you smell of death; ergo you are dead. Whatever name you once had belongs to the past. Therefore, to be perfectly grammatically correct, we must say that you had a name."

"I'm… not dead."

"That's just what a dead person would say."

"Just look at me. I'm talking to you! I'm walking around!"

"Eh? I've seen corpses in a lot worse shape than you are up and dancing the Charleston."

"What's the Charleston?"

"You don't know? Why, what year is it?"

Emma felt a hand on her shoulder. She turned to see Riley join her. Riley pushed their glasses up onto their nose and answered the wizard in a lecture-room voice. "We seem to have a misunderstanding. You say you smell death; ergo Emma must be dead?"

"Quite so."

"Are there no other factors that could account for the odor?"

Merlin cocked his head and cleaned out an ear with his finger. "Highly unlikely! Highly."

"But possible."

"Yes, if you want to be nitpicky. There are certain people, touched by otherworldly forces, who stink of the dead, who draw the dead to them and make them tell their tales. But I haven't met anyone like that in cen— Well, in a good long time. Unless…" The wizard squinted, then drew out a pair of spectacles and donned them. He looked down his nose at Emma. "What's your name, girl?"

"Emma."

"No, tell me your family name."

"Day."

"Not on your father's side. On your mother's."

"It's Barrow."

Merlin staggered back like he'd been slapped in the face. He shook his head and put away his spectacles. "The name is familiar to me. Your family is known to deal with the dead."

"That's a pretty dramatic way of putting it."

"I would argue that necromancy is a pretty dramatic career choice!"

Necromancy? Did this Merlin guy think she brought the dead back to life or something? The spirits who came to her were normal people, just a little more transparent. Did they really leave an odor behind that Merlin could smell? Or was it more likely that he was making things up to make himself into a real, grandiose Wizard of Oz figure? Emma felt jumpy. She wanted to either walk away or let it rip. Neither of those options would get her what she needed though. She gritted her teeth and looked Merlin in the eye. "Regardless of what you think of my… career choice, I think we can all agree that I am not, at present, dead. We came here to ask you about a coin that I suspect has magical properties. Orion said you were an expert in such things. Will you help us?"

"That very much depends on the type of coin and the type of magic. Do you have it with you?"

Emma reached out and opened her hand. The gold coin she'd removed from the fairy's lips lay flat on her palm.

Merlin eyed the coin like it was a rattlesnake. He looked at it from the left side, and then he walked around to the right, where he bent down and examined it at eye level. He raised his hand, pinched his thumb and forefinger together, then quick as blinking your eye, snagged the coin from Emma's palm.

"Now who's being dramatic?" Emma said.

"One can never be too careful with these things," Merlin said. "When magic's at play, the force of the entire cosmos might be compressed into a single grain of sand. Let's have a look." He held the coin up to the light. "Late Roman. Caligula, judging by the sneer. He debased the currency, you know. I'd be surprised if this coin is even half gold."

"Then I guess it's not that valuable?"

"Oh no, it's extremely valuable. With ancient coins, you see, the value doesn't come from the metal they're made of. No, no. The value comes from their rarity. And this coin is exceedingly rare. They had so little gold, people melted them down to make drinking goblets. Of course, people didn't care so much about lead poising back then."

"How many coins like this are still around?"

Merlin furrowed his brow and scratched his bearded chin. "Why, that's a very good question. Let me see." He stood, then walked to the back of the tent, behind one of the piles of junk. Something shifted, and then there was the clatter of metal falling to the floor. A hubcap rolled out, circled, and came to a stop in front of Emma's feet. A few moments later, the wizard emerged. He carried an enormous book, which he dropped onto the coffee table with a thud.

The book measured over two feet tall and at least a foot thick. It was bound in thick russet leather that cracked and flaked along the spine. Tall Gothic letters, gilded and embossed, filled the front cover: COINS OF THE WORLD. Merlin flipped the book open and thumbed through the pages. They weren't typical book pages. They were made of a stiff, transparent material that wasn't quite plastic. Each page contained two dozen small pockets. Most pockets contained a single coin. The rest were empty.

"We have Caesar and Augustus, then Gaius, Drusus, Hadrian—lovely wall he built—then Tiberius, Augustus, and… Caligula." He hovered over the book like a heron scanning the water for fish, then he deftly extracted a small coin from the book and held it up for Emma to see.

"It's… the same. How many coins like that are there?"

"What? Oh yes, you did want to know that." He slipped the coin back into its place, then tapped his index finger on several other pockets while mumbling under his breath. "One, two, three, four. Plus, the one she has, and another two auctioned in the seventies. Why yes, I believe that's it." He looked up, smiling. "Seven."

"You're telling me that there are only seven of these coins in existence?"

"Yes."

"And you own four of them?"

"Yes."

"Why?"

"The rarer the coin, the easier it is to enchant." Merlin said it like it was the most obvious thing in the world.

"And… is this coin enchanted?"

Merlin brought the coin just under his nose, then sniffed. He lowered his brow in concentration, then stuck out his tongue and touched the very tip of it to the coin. "Most definitely." He frowned and smacked his lips like he'd just tasted something bitter. "Juniper and cardamom. You know what that means."

"No."

"Really?" He returned the coin to Emma. "What are they teaching in school these days? Everyone knows that binding spells taste of juniper and trapping spells smell of cardamom."

"Binding and trapping." Emma frowned in thought.

"If I may ask, where did you find this coin?"

"On the body of a… fairy." Even though she was talking with a guy named Merlin, part of Emma still cringed at saying the f-word to this relative stranger. She was still getting used to the idea of fairies being real, not to mention wizards. "It was on her lips. When I picked the coin up, she started glowing, then disappeared."

"That makes perfect sense. Fairies and their brethren do not belong on this earthly plain. They can only come here through an effort of will, either their own or that of a summoner. If a fairy is here of her own accord and perishes, her body will be drawn back to the fae realm just as water sinks to the lowest point."

Emma began to see where he was leading. "Whoever killed her put a binding spell on the coin. That must be why her body didn't return to the fae realm when she died."

"Yes, quite so. And the trapping spell would have triggered when you picked up the coin, breaking the binding and causing the fairy to disappear." Merlin suddenly frowned. "I hope it wasn't anyone I know. Humans are used to death, but creatures like fairies and the fae? It's quite rare."

"Her name was Isolde," Emma said.

"Oh dear." Merlin chewed on his beard. "They finally got her, did they? I worried for her, you know. She didn't always see the sharks she swam with."

"Who are the sharks?"

"No." Merlin shook his head. "You must not get involved, child. No matter what you felt for poor Isolde, you mustn't. Dangerous, inhuman forces are at play. Powerful foes are crashing together like icebergs in a glacial floe. If you were to try to stop them or even alter their course, you'd be crushed and the powers wouldn't even notice."

A lump formed in Emma's throat. She tried to swallow it, but her mouth was sandy and dry. She'd been sent here to solve a murder. It was never easy to crack a case, but she'd done it five times before, and she felt she knew the ropes. But things were different here. She didn't know anything about the players, about the lay of the land. She wanted more than anything to call it quits, to go find Sassy and drive back home and chase away the dread with a cup of hot cocoa. But her dad's life was at stake. If she didn't solve this case for the fae, she might never see him again. He might die in the fae realm assuming he'd been forgotten and abandoned. No. That was not acceptable. She looked the wizard dead in the eye. "You say I shouldn't get involved, but I already am. I work on behalf of the fae prince, Elric. Isolde was his sister."

"Elric. There's a name I haven't heard in ages." He grimaced. "No wonder you smell of death. The fae prince walks the earth again, and you serve him?"

"I don't serve him. He's a monster. I… I hate him! But he's taken my father."

"Indeed. Elric was never above taking hostages. Still, I must ask, would your father wish you to be facing such terrible danger on his behalf?"

"I don't know," Emma said. "I don't even know what kind of danger you're talking about. No one will tell me!"

The old wizard sighed and gestured to the armchairs. "Sit. You are my guests. I will tell you what you wish to know, but first, would you care for refreshments? I believe I have a tea service filed somewhere next to the toolboxes. He tilted his head to his right, where a mountain of rusty toolboxes looked like it was ready to collapse.

"No, thank you," Emma said. She chose a high-backed chair with worn russet leather padding and polished mahogany armrests inlaid with carvings of lions. She sat on it, and the cushion wheezed. The surrounding air smelled like beeswax and vanilla. It was comfortable, almost too much so and combined with the warmth from the fire made her feel drowsy. "We just had tea at Orion's, and I'm dying to know what the heck is going on around here. Someone told us that Isolde had enemies among her kind, and you just said powerful interests are colliding. But nobody will tell me exactly what that means!"

"Small wonder," Merlin said. He sat in the chair closest to the fire, kicked his feet up, and basked in the warmth. "If there's one thing the wizarding game teaches you, child, it's the power of a good secret. Under normal circumstances, I'd throw you out and tell you never to speak the name Isolde again. But your story about your father tugs at my heartstrings, dusty as they might be. What do you know about Isolde?"

"Only what I told you. She's a fairy princess. The fae prince calls her sister. I don't know if it's biological since they seem to be different species."

"You'll be better served if you forget biology for now. The rules of our world don't apply to the fae, the fairies, or any of their kind. The same thing goes for objects. While an earthly flute may invite the listener to dance. A fae flute compels them. An earthly mirror reflects an image inverted in space, but a fae mirror reflects an image inverted in time."

"They're objects of power."

"You can imagine how valuable such objects would be here on earth."

"I've seen people killed for them."

"Indeed. I suspect you've seen a fairy killed for them as well. Fairies flit easily between realms. They're the perfect couriers, bringing items of power to earth to trade."

Emma recoiled. There was one thing she knew the fae wanted: humans. They'd staffed the Evening Palace with zombified slaves. They'd fed on them too, slowly draining their life force until there was nothing left. "They trade people."

Merlin laughed. "Thankfully, they cannot. But they do lust after the products of humanity. You see, the fae are like fire.

They can only consume, never create. They have no art, no theater, no music of their own."

"But when I was taken to their realm, they had a ball in a beautiful castle, with music and dancing and a banquet."

"And who prepared the banquet?"

"Human chefs."

"What about the orchestra?"

"I didn't get a good look."

"I guarantee that the orchestra was human. I guarantee that human artisans built their beautiful castle, painted their beautiful murals, sewed their shining clothes. But this approach only goes so far. Most of their prisoners were taken in centuries past. There's no way for them to reproduce a popular movie or video game."

"Video game? Wait just a second. Are you telling me that the fairies are out here trading magical items for video games?"

"Yes, and for DVDs, CDs, and novels. Anything that the human mind creates. To the fae, a box set of *Buffy the Vampire Slayer* is as rare and as valuable as a magical flute would be on earth. Isolde was one of many fairies who facilitate such trades."

As she listened, Emma spun the Caligula coin in her fingers. It all made a weird kind of sense. She grew up in the eighties, during the final days of the Soviet Union. She'd watched a TV show once about a man who smuggled blue jeans into Moscow and sold them for hundreds of dollars. Scarcity could turn even the most ordinary objects into luxury items. And wherever there was smuggling, you were sure to find organized crime. "Tell me, have you ever heard of the Cappotelli crime family?"

Merlin's already pale face got even whiter. He turned his head and glanced at the door, as if checking to see if anyone watched. "Who do you think runs the faire?"

"Hold on a second," Emma said, throwing her hands in

front of her. "I thought what's-his-name, Griffin, owned the faire."

Merlin, his small eyes sparking, appeared to enjoy the role of teacher. "He owns it, yes, and I suppose he's ultimately responsible for booking attractions, collecting tickets, and stage-managing silly things like the annual coronation of the Emerald King or Queen. But that's not what I'm referring to with the Cappotellis."

"Griffin handles the ordinary, aboveboard stuff, and the Cappotellis manage the black market of magical items? It seems like a strange racket for the mob."

"Is it though?" Merlin asked. "Sicily is known for two things: their Mafias and their *streghe*. Is it so surprising that they'd eventually think to combine the two?"

"Streghe?"

"Witches."

"You're telling me that the Cappotellis are a magical Mafia?"

"Not *a* magical Mafia," Merlin said. "*The* magical Mafia."

CHAPTER 15
LEGENDS

Merlin stood to put away his coins. Emma, Riley, and Orion sat in the dusty armchairs in front of the blazing wood stove. The air smelled of smoke, old leather, and musky herbs. Emma leaned back and tried to make sense of what she'd just heard.

Linda Cappotelli, her client, was not only born into the Mafia, but into magic as well. Emma wished she could say it didn't make sense, but the more she thought about it, the more it did. It explained why Linda had been so confident in Emma's abilities to summon her father's spirit. It explained how Linda had seemed to sense the spirit's presence, even if she couldn't see or speak with him.

"I guess we solved one mystery. We know why the Mafia heiress came to Seattle. If her family runs the shadier side of the faire, it makes sense they would have people on the ground. Except"—doubt gnawed at Emma's heart—"Linda told me that she rejected the illegal side of her family's business, that she was a legitimate businesswoman."

"Legality and morality are two separate things," Riley said.

"You're right. Smuggling magical items into this world seems shady, but is it illegal?"

"How could it be? Only a handful of people know that it's possible," Riley said.

"I wonder if the same thing is true for magic in general. It's not illegal to—I don't know—turn someone into a frog. If anyone tried to make it illegal, they'd be laughed out of Congress." Emma turned to Merlin. "Do you know anything about this?"

Merlin was digging through his many scarves, apparently searching for something. He looked up. "What? Laws? Don't be ridiculous. There are no human laws that govern magic."

"What about magical creatures like fairies? Laws about murder only apply to humans, don't they? Killing a fairy wouldn't, strictly speaking, be against the law."

"It wouldn't, at least not in the human realm," Merlin replied. He sucked in his chin and started looking through his scarves again.

Emma went silent as doubt gnawed a pit in her stomach. What was Linda Cappotelli capable of? Could she or her people have murdered Isolde in a magic deal gone wrong? Could they have enchanted the coin and placed it on her lips to keep her in the human realm long enough for someone to find her? Could they have wanted to send a message? To whom? How could Emma prove it?

It wouldn't do any good to approach Linda directly. Emma couldn't expect the Mafia heiress to tell her the truth. No, it would be better to approach someone on the periphery. Someone who might have an axe to grind.

"We need to talk to Richard Griffin."

"I found it!" Merlin said, pulling a slender metal chain from between his layers of scarves. It was like a magic trick in a Vegas show. No matter how much he pulled, the chain kept coming and coming. It splashed onto the floor and piled up around Merlin's feet. Then he reached the end. He unclipped a small circular silver object and handed it to Emma, then began stuffing the chain back into his scarves.

It was a plain flat disk, as big around as a silver dollar but thicker. It had no ornamentation and nothing to indicate its purpose except for a groove running around its perimeter and a small semicircular clip on the top. "What is it?"

"What?" Merlin looked up, startled. He regarded Emma with a confused expression, and then his eyes lit up with recognition. "Oh that? Open it."

Emma fit her thumbnail into the groove on the side of the object. It popped open to reveal something that looked like a watch except that its face was completely blank and it only had one hand, which pointed toward the door. "It's a compass? There's no marking for north."

"It's not that kind of compass," Merlin said. "It doesn't care a whit about north or south. It leads you where you need to go."

"This will help us find Griffin?"

"If you need to find Mr. Griffin, yes."

"How do I... tell it what I need?"

"Tell it?" Merlin looked perplexed. "Why, you don't tell it anything, child. It knows. It simply knows!"

Emma looked again at the compass, and a feeling of unease climbed her spine. At a glance, the thing appeared harmless enough, but the more she looked at it, the more it seemed... off. It was oddly heavy and its metal oddly dull. Its needle didn't wobble like a normal compass. It only moved when she did, reorienting itself subtly to point toward the door. "Is this... an object of power? Was it smuggled in from the fae realm?"

Merlin let out a hooting laugh. "Do you think I'd give such a thing away so easily? No, child. It's no fae device. It's simple, everyday magic. I... tend to forget things, to walk into a room and have no idea what I came for. I made this compass for myself years ago, to always point toward my destination."

"Don't… you need it, then?"

"I never use the thing."

"Why?"

"I never remember to!"

———

Emma shivered as they exited the tent into the dark alley. During their chat with Merlin, evening had turned to night, and a chill set in. The air was filled with the scent of roasted meat, apples, and corn on the cob. On the other side of the tents, the coronation party raged. A musical group played a fiddle-and-drum tune while people clapped in unison. There was a whoosh, and fire lit the sky to their left, and then the crowd cheered.

"Aww, man," Orion said. "Nessa's going to be mad at me. She wanted to see the fire-eaters. I better get back and watch the store so she can catch the show."

"Thanks, Orion," Emma said. "I owe you one." She looked at him standing there in his robes, wearing too many crystal necklaces. Regardless of what she'd thought of Orion before, he'd really come through for her tonight.

"Catch you on the flip side!" he said, disappearing into the night.

Emma took the magic compass from her pocket and flipped it open. Riley edged closer. "When this is all over, I'd love to have my team take that thing apart and see how it works."

"You don't know? I almost expected you to rattle off chapter and verse." Emma pretended to push glasses up her nose. "It's a simple geolocating spell, first mentioned in *Ranchard's Arcane Compendium*, although my sources say he stole it from his butler…"

Riley smiled and lightly punched Emma's shoulder. "You're wrong on three points. First, there's no such thing as *Ranchard's Arcane Compendium*. Second, I know surprisingly little about magic. If you want to know about demons, I can help you. The fae? Sure. Ghosts? Of course. But magic? Like the witches-and-wizards-hocus-pocus stuff?"

"Specifically, magic-compass stuff."

"My academic field, applied folklore, doesn't deal with it."

"Why not?"

"It's so rare it might as well not be real. Too much folklore, and not enough application."

"What about my aunt Coralee? She cast a love spell. I'm pretty sure it worked."

"Emma, it drove the guy crazy and cursed the neighborhood for forty years."

"Details."

"I don't know what Merlin's deal is. I don't know if he really can work magic or if he's just a crazy old man with a tent full of junk. But I do know that if this compass works, it's beyond anything that I've ever studied."

"What do you say we take it for a spin? Mr. Griffin is bound to be nearby. If anyone can tell us about the Cappotellis' involvement in the fair, it will be him."

———

The compass led them out of the dark alley, back onto the cobblestone thoroughfare lit by fairy lights overhead. It led them away from the raucous music, from the smell of sizzling meat and the cheers. It led them past a fenced-in staging area where a welder in an archer costume repaired an excavator's bucket as the welding rig shot orange sparks into the dark sky. It led them to a quiet cul-de-sac ringed with half-timbered Tudor structures, or at least imitations of them. On at least one building, the plaster had chipped and fallen away to reveal chicken wire and plywood beneath.

This area of the fair, Emma decided, must be for more daytime use. She and Riley were the only people on the street. All the buildings were shuttered, with no lights in their tiny windows, except for one, with electric light blazing. Emma checked the compass. It pointed directly at the building. They followed it to the front door but stopped when they heard voices inside.

"You fail to understand that the faire is a meeting place, neutral ground." It sounded like Mr. Griffin. "While your… organization has had sole access for several years, you don't have a monopoly. You have no right to shut out competitors. Remember who it is that owns the land? Such legalities mean a great deal to the, ah, people with whom you do business."

A woman's voice replied, a low voice that tugged at Emma's memory. "Of course it's important, Richard. Why do you think I'm speaking with you instead of taking matters into my own hands?"

"That would be unwise."

"My question to you is this: what's your number?"

"My number?" Mr. Griffin said.

"We're both pragmatic people. Neither of us was born yesterday. You've let us operate out of the faire for the past decade. We've established many unique connections. This has paid dividends for both of us. Your faire is now the biggest in the world. I won't ask how much profit you make."

"Yes, we've both done well," Mr. Griffin said. "Why change things? Why rock the boat? I'm perfectly happy to run the fair and to look the other way while your organization makes its deals."

"You mean you want to look the other way while those… fools try to destroy what we've built?"

"I hardly see why any of this is my problem."

"Then you're blind." A chair slid across the floor. "You

have until tomorrow to consider my proposal. If we're not able to reach an agreement, my organization will have to take whatever action it deems necessary to protect its interests."

"Is that a threat?"

"Please, Richard, don't sound so offended. You know as well as I do that nobody's clean. Everyone has something to hide. Especially someone with a squeaky-clean, family-friendly image to protect. But secrets are pesky things, aren't they? They have a way of being found. The Cappotelli family is good at finding things."

Emma heard footsteps across a hardwood floor. Then the door opened. The light from inside spilled around the figure of a woman who stormed past them before Emma could see her face. Emma turned to watch her walk away. She wore a long tan overcoat with white chinos and a cherry-red purse. A shiver ran up Emma's spine. Was that Linda? If so, what did her presence mean? Had she recognized Emma? What had she meant when she talked about protecting her organization's interests?

"Excuse me? Can I help you?" A bewildered-looking Mr. Griffin stood in the open door. He had taken off his jacket, and his white button-down was open at the collar. He looked at Emma and Riley, then down at the volunteer passes around their necks, and then a look of recognition lit up his face. "Didn't I tell you to return your volunteer passes at the main entrance? I don't need them."

"We're not here about the passes," Emma said. "We're here about the dead fairy in the time capsule."

"Oh, are you?" His expression was a challenge. "Why should I talk to you about anything?"

"Because we're working on behalf of Isolde's family, trying to find her killer. Since your business depends on trust and goodwill from both human and not-so-human people, it's in your best interest to help me."

Griffin let out an exhausted sigh. "I guess you'd better come in."

While the building might have looked like a medieval house from the outside, inside it was a modern, messy office, albeit one with a wood-burning fireplace. The room was lit by four fluorescent fixtures bolted to the ceiling. One wall was taken up by a bank of gray filing cabinets and a university-sized whiteboard covered in pink and yellow sticky notes. Another wall was covered in old banners from the faire in years gone by. An open closet door revealed stacks of crumbling brown banker's boxes. In the center of the room sat a large oak desk holding an out-of-date computer monitor and large piles of old, yellowed papers.

Griffin gestured for them to sit. He took a seat behind the desk, laced his fingers behind his head, and leaned back. His chair spring squealed. "So you know about Isolde."

"We found her."

"Didn't I tell you to stay away from the work crew by the world tree? But then again, you aren't normal volunteers, are you? Normal volunteers don't have founder passes." He pointed at the charm dangling from Emma's neck. "Normal volunteers don't know about fairies."

"Why did you tell us to avoid the time capsule? Did you know that Isolde was inside?"

Griffin paused for a moment, jaw hanging open, and then his face turned beet red. "What's in the water tonight? Is it a full moon? First that thing happened to poor Isolde. Then the time capsule was empty. Then that woman comes into my office and threatens me. Then two fake volunteers barge in and accuse me of murder!"

"You invited us in!" Emma said. "And I'm not accusing you of anything. But you must admit it's a pretty big coincidence. Maybe you can explain to me why you didn't want us near the time capsule then."

"It was supposed to be a surprise! We spent a lot of money

hyping the blasted thing. You must have heard the radio ads. 'Secrets? Jewels? What will be revealed inside the founders' time capsule?'"

"I don't listen to radio."

"She doesn't listen to the radio," he said, rolling his eyes. "Let me tell you, a lot of people do! Ticket sales are through the roof, but I'm not even sure it's worth it. People have been sneaking around all day, slipping into staff-only areas, trying to peek at the thing. One guy even climbed the clock tower with a huge pair of binoculars!"

"Did you give all of them volunteer passes?"

Griffin shrugged. "They claim to be volunteers when we catch them. What should we do? Call the cops? It's easier to call their bluff, give them a pass, and send them off to hard labor. The faire always needs volunteers."

It was unorthodox, sure, but it made a kind of sense. "Let's move on to the time capsule itself. It was empty."

"You think I don't know?" He rolled his eyes. "It was a disaster! Worse than someone getting a peek inside and spilling the beans. We brought all these people in, expecting a big surprise. To give them zilch, zero, a big fat nothingburger? They'd tear the place apart!"

Emma thought back to the scene outside, full of music and laughter. "The crowds didn't seem that upset to me."

"I bet they didn't."

"Why not?"

"When I saw that the time capsule was empty, I did the only thing I could think of."

"Which was?"

"I lied. I filled up a laundry basket with emerald tokens, and we threw them out at the crowd. At the faire, that stuff is as good as cash, so people were too busy scrambling for the things to wonder what kind of weirdo uses a laundry basket for a time capsule."

Emma laughed. "And that worked?"

"I'm still alive, aren't I? The faire is still standing, isn't it? Everybody rushed out to spend their newfound riches on beer and turkey legs. I bet they're having a hell of a party. Too bad I'm the one who's going to have a hangover. I must have lost fifty grand back there."

Emma winced. Fifty grand was a lot of money. And who knew how much the missing time capsule contents were worth? "Did you really think there were secrets and jewels inside the time capsule?"

"Who would bury a bunch of jewels in the woods for thirty years? All that was just razzle dazzle, you know, salesmanship. The truth is, I didn't have a clue. The founders put it there."

"You're not one of the founders?"

Griffin laughed. "No, I'm a businessman, a general contractor. The founders might have dreamed up the faire, but I built it."

"You knew them then."

"Whatever you've heard about the founders, take it with a grain of salt. There're a lot of tall tales floating around, a lot of myths."

Emma remembered the tall guard in chain mail, who had been overawed by her founder pass. "Someone told me that they were supposed to return in the hour of the faire's greatest need."

"That's exactly what I mean. Baloney."

"How do you know?"

"Because I made up that story. I made up most of the secrets you hear people whisper about the founders. People eat it up. They retell the stories and make up new ones. You can't buy that kind of marketing."

"What's the truth then?"

He let out a sigh and absentmindedly began cleaning his fingernails. "Same as most creatives. The founders were artists and visionaries but not very practical. This place, this whole park, was a place for them to escape into. They kept it going for a while, but then money got low, and the wolf came knocking. They sold the whole kit and caboodle to me. That's when we made the founder passes, like the one around your neck."

"Are they still involved in the faire?"

"They haven't been around for years. A couple live out on the Olympic Peninsula. A couple moved to Florida. I don't keep track of them. Besides, the world's changed. Those guys, they really wanted to be knights in shining armor. They wouldn't understand what goes on here with the fantasy stuff and people like Isolde."

People like Isolde. Emma got the impression that he wasn't referring to the fact that Isolde was a fairy. He meant her job as a courier between realms, the job that could have gotten her killed. Emma's stomach was full of butterflies. She'd asked plenty of questions so far, but not the one she really cared about. It was time to change that. She looked Griffin in the eye, ready to gauge his reaction. "I saw Linda Cappotelli leaving your office."

"Did you?" He shrugged and yawned, but his beady eyes focused sharply on Emma. "What's your point? Isolde's people deal with them all the time."

"Were the Cappotellis in conflict with Isolde?"

"I keep my nose out of that kind of thing."

"But if you had to guess?"

"Everybody knew Isolde."

"I heard she had problems."

"We've all got problems."

"I heard she and the Emerald Queen were fighting."

"Ezell has a temper."

"I heard other players were edging in on her business."

"You've heard a lot of things."

"Just now, I heard Linda Cappotelli trying to negotiate a

deal for exclusive access to the paranormal smuggling channels at the faire."

Griffin laughed, but his eyes stayed hard. "Trespassing and eavesdropping. Don't you think that's a lot to pack into one night?"

"Linda said another group is edging in on her business. Who is it?"

"I prefer not to say."

"I need you to tell me."

Griffin stood. "This conversation is over."

"Let me say it more clearly," Emma said, still in her chair. "The fae prince, Elric, needs you to tell me. If word gets back to him that you're stonewalling my investigation, he can stop the magical smuggling trade in its tracks. I can't imagine that would be good for your bottom line."

Griffin sighed and looked at Emma. There were daggers in his eyes. "You don't realize the situation you're putting me in. I'll tell you what you want to know under one condition."

"Name it."

"No one can know you heard from me, and I never want to see you again. When your little investigation is done, I want you to turn in your founder pass at the gate and never come back."

"That's four conditions."

"Do you accept?"

Emma examined Mr. Griffin's portly face, his red cheeks, and his small intense eyes. What was he scared of? She doubted he would tell her, and anyway, the deal seemed like a fair one. "I accept."

"It's… the Fairykin." He grimaced. "Most people come to the faire, play dress-up, then go back to their normal lives. But the Fairykin aren't right in the head. They're not just pretending to be fairies; they want to be fairies. They live together, change their names, wear the wings year-round. At first I thought it was just a couple of harmless nutjobs, but every year more and more of them show up. They already voted in their queen. Now they're making a play to control a piece of the black market."

Emma's mouth hung open. The Fairykin? She had a million questions but didn't know where to start. She picked one at random. "Do you know if—"

"We're done."

"But I just—"

"I lived up to my end of our agreement. I answered your question. Now it's time for you to honor yours and get out of my office." He pointed toward the door.

CHAPTER 16
BROCHURE

They stepped out of Griffin's office onto the dark cobblestone cul-de-sac. In the distance, the music had gotten louder, the cheers brighter and punctuated by the festive crack of fireworks. Riley wheeled around and faced Emma, their mouth drawn to a tight line.

"I can't believe you agreed to those terms!" Riley's face was red, and they vibrated with barely contained emotion.

Emma froze, confused. The terms? It seemed reasonable to keep quiet about Griffin's involvement in their investigation. And if he didn't want to see them again, it wasn't like Emma could force him to. As much as she tried, Emma couldn't figure out what had upset Riley so much. She raised the palms of her hands in the universal gesture for *don't shoot*. "What's going on? What terms?"

"What terms? You said once you found Isolde's killer, we'll never come to the faire again."

"Did I say that?" Emma's heart sank. Riley loved the faire and came every year. Had Emma just bargained that away without a thought? Guilt blossomed in her stomach, and spread out, making her whole body heavy. "I'm sorry. I was so focused on the investigation."

"I'm not saying you were wrong."

"But I *was* wrong."

"What I mean is that this investigation, finding the killer, saving your dad—it's all so much more important than my hobbies. But it would have been nice if you consulted me. If I'm going to give something up, I'd like to have a choice, you know?"

"I do. I'm sorry. Maybe… maybe the situation's not so black-and-white. I'm the one who made the agreement never to come back. Griffin can't expect you to live by it. If you come back next year, you'll just be another face in the crowd. You'll be wearing a different costume. How would he recognize you?"

"I… guess you have a point." Riley's features softened.

"I still should have asked you."

The two of them stood quietly in the cull-de-sac. A crisp breeze blew by, rustling the tree branches overhead. It brought the scents of wood smoke, grilling meats, tart berry pies, sweet cotton candy and deep-fried funnel cakes. Emma's stomach growled. "I guess we forgot dinner."

"I guess we did."

"What do you say we head over to the food vendors and grab something?" She held up her wallet, which contained her emerald tokens. "My treat."

"Okay… but I'll warn you, I'm getting dessert."

They started back the way they'd come, moving toward the lights, the noise, the delicious smells of food. Emma still nursed a tender spot in her heart where the guilt had wounded her. She glanced at Riley and wondered what they were thinking. They didn't seem mad, just thoughtful. With a little time and a little food and a pinch of luck, things would be okay. Then they could come together and plan the next part of the investigation.

It didn't take long to reach the food court. The savory smells blended and overwhelmed the senses. The chatter of a thousand private conversations merged into a roar. Emma craned her neck to get the lay of the land. Whoever built the place took the phrase *food court* a little too literally. At its far end was a small platform on which sat a table and an elaborately carved chair. It was obviously meant for the Emerald Queen, though it was currently vacant. In front of the platform, an enormous dining area sprawled, surrounded by white-tented food stalls. A dozen long rows of tables and benches spilled over with fairgoers swilling enormous tankards, eating soup from sourdough trenchers, and gnawing on giant turkey legs.

Emma took the emerald tokens from her wallet, divided them into two equal stacks, and handed one to Riley. "What do you say we get our food, then meet back here to find a place to sit?"

"Sounds good." Riley smiled. Things seemed to be okay.

After Riley wandered off, Emma just looked at the food court, trying to figure out her options. The turkey leg booth was a short walk away, with a short line. Behind the counter, a kind of Ferris wheel of poultry slowly spun while bathed in flame from both sides. Juices dripped from the golden-brown meat, sizzled, and sent up a smoke that made Emma's mouth water. It seemed obligatory to get one. Still, the more Emma took in their absolute girth, the more doubt assailed her. Did she really want to dig in to a messy, dripping piece of meat in public? The last time she'd eaten turkey, she'd fallen asleep in front of the TV. But now, with so much work to do, she needed to be alert.

The next stall she stopped at sold French onion soup in sourdough trenchers, smothered in gruyère cheese, and toasted until it bubbled and turned golden brown. Not only did this seem like a more sensible option than the turkey leg, but there was also zero waste. When you finished the soup, you simply ate the bread. Nice and neat. Emma got in line.

The mood was light at the food court as people happily

spent the emerald tokens they'd gotten for free at the coronation. None of the crowd seemed to know that a body had been discovered only a few minutes' walk away. Emma wished she could be one of them, to enjoy herself without the weight of the world on her shoulders.

"Emma?" a woman said.

Emma noticed for the first time that she recognized the woman in front of her in line. "Vanessa?" When Emma had first met her, she'd worked at the diner. Her dirty-blond hair had been up, and she'd worn the same powder-blue dress that all the waitresses wore. Emma could hardly believe it was the same person standing before her. This Vanessa seemed younger and more relaxed. Her hair was down, and she wore simple robes like Orion's. "How have you been? I'm sorry we didn't get a chance to talk earlier."

"It's no problem. You seemed busy, talking with that guy about the fairy." She leaned in. "Tell me, is that stuff real? Like, really real? I don't mean to be a killjoy or anything, but after Orion's vampire thing…"

Emma nodded. It made sense for Vanessa to be skeptical. After all, Orion had been so convinced that vampires were out to get him, he'd packed up his store and fled town. Emma sighed. "I hate to say it, but the fairy stuff is real. One of the fairies that works the faire was killed today."

"Get out of here! For real?"

"For really real," Emma said. "I have to find the killer."

"How? I mean, how do you even do that?" A note of awe ringed Vanessa's voice.

"I'm still figuring it out. So far, it seems like any other investigation. People tell you little nuggets of information. You follow up on them, talk with more people, and hope that it all comes together in the end."

"Too much stress for me."

"Me too." Emma moaned. "You have no idea how complicated this place is. Sure, it looks like a relaxing time playing make believe in the woods. But there are layers inside layers. I thought I knew what was going on, but I just found out I need to look into a group of fairy impersonators called the Fairykin."

Vanessa's face lit up. "The Fairykin? Have you seen the queen? She's so pretty, and she has the most amazing crown. It's metal, but it's made in the shape of, like, branches woven together."

"See?" Emma said. "You know way more about them than I do. All I know is that they're weirdos who are trying to be fairies."

"Where did you hear that?"

"I'm not allowed to say. Why do you ask?"

"A couple of them came into the shop today, and we started talking. They said they weren't trying to be fairies. Said it was more of a spiritual connection to the idea of fairies."

Emma struggled to process what she'd just heard. "The idea of fairies?"

"Isn't it so cool? They said fairies are beings of love and light, and anyone who's willing to purify themselves can learn to commune with the fairy realm. They hold a service every Friday night at the old Masonic temple in Freemont."

"Like, church services?"

"Don't be silly. More like people getting in touch with the fairies together. Doesn't it sound amazing?"

It sounded like a cult. What had Griffin said? Every year more and more Fairykin arrived at the faire. That wasn't an accident. Emma would bet her whole stack of emerald tokens that those Fairykin hadn't really been shopping for crystals in Orion's tent. They were recruiting, and they must have seen an easy target in Vanessa. "Did they tell you anything else about the group?"

"I don't think so, no. But they did leave a pamphlet about the Friday meetings." Vanessa opened the small tan bag she carried, dug around, then pulled out a bent and tattered slip of glossy paper. It had been folded in thirds, and on the front was a logo in the shape of purple fairy wings and text, in a vaguely Middle Eastern font, reading FAIRIES AND YOU.

Emma's jaw hung open. They had pamphlets. She didn't know why that shocked her, but it did. The Fairykin, a group of fairy impersonators, had pamphlets and a weekly meeting. What else did they have? A website? A toll-free line?

"All right, ladies, what's it going to be?" a gruff voice said. They had made it to the front of the line. "We have anything your little hearts desire as long as it's onion soup."

Emma shook her head, trying to force herself back to the present moment. She looked around desperately for a menu, but there was only the vendor with his three-day stubble and stained white apron. "I guess I'll have the onion soup?"

"We got two sizes. Big or little."

"Big."

"With the cheese or without?"

"With."

"That'll be five emerald tokens."

Emma gasped. "That's twenty-five dollars! I thought everything here was supposed to cost one token."

"Inflation." The man shrugged. "Take it up with the UN."

"Fine." Emma counted out five tokens and exchanged them for a piping hot trencher of soup crusted over with melted gruyère. It looked good, but did it look twenty-five-dollars good? Her mouth didn't care. She started salivating.

After Vanessa was served, the two of them headed back toward the food court entrance. "I'm going to meet up with Riley and find a table. Would you like to join us?"

"Thanks, but I've got my work cut out for me back at the crystal shop. Between you and me, Orion's kind of helpless when it comes to keeping the shop clean and pleasant for customers. I don't know how he ran his store for so long without me."

"Before you go, could I ask you a favor?"

"Sure."

"Could I borrow the pamphlet? I promise I'll give it back."

"Of course." Vanessa handed it to her. "Keep it. I already read it."

————

Emma found Riley waiting at the meeting spot, holding a bundle of fragrant hand pies like it was a baby. They leaned against a fence post, looking idly at the stream of fairgoers walking by. Their expression was blank. Was it boredom? Or anger? Riley looked up at Emma and smiled. What a relief!

"I'm glad you're here. I'm starving. I've been scoping out this table over here, and nobody seems to be using it."

"You won't believe what I just found out," Emma said, holding the pamphlet up. "The Fairykin are some kind of cult, and they tried to recruit Vanessa."

"Really?" Riley's brow furrowed. "A cult that venerates fairies? Of course there's nothing more natural than for minor cults to spring up around local deities. The Greeks had the cult of Eleusis. The Celts had a special god for every tree, hill, and stream in the forest. But—"

"Hey, before you go all professor mode, do you mind if we grab that table? This soup's starting to burn my hand."

"What? Oh yeah, sorry." Riley led Emma to the free table, nearly losing her pies after tripping on a cable. Fortunately, they recovered in time to spill them onto the whitewashed tabletop. "As I was saying, it's not uncommon for little cults to spring up around certain… entities. But they always tend to be around a specific entity. I've never heard of a cult venerating an entire species."

Emma cocked her head and looked at Riley. Over the year and a half since they'd met, Emma had come to not only respect Riley but to love them as a friend. But loving someone doesn't mean you understand them. "That's what strikes you as the strangest thing about the Fairykin? That they're into fairies as a species, rather than a single, particular fairy?"

"Of course." Riley took a bite from a small meat pie. "Was there something else that stood out to you?"

"How about… everything?" Emma unpacked her trencher, napkins, and plastic spoon. She was just about to dig in when an idea slapped her in the face. "How about the fact that Ezell, queen of the Fairykin, was seen in a screaming fight with Isolde, an actual fairy?"

"That is odd," Riley said around a bite of pie. They swallowed. "If the Fairykin do, indeed, venerate fairies, one would think they would behave respectfully toward them."

"One would think."

Emma picked up her spoon and dug into the trencher of soup. The spoon broke through the gooey cheese, and the air soon filled with the mouth-watering smell of caramelized onions, garlic, and tarragon. Emma collected a perfect bite of soup and cheese and bread and put it in her mouth. It immediately warmed her to the core. It was a wonderful counterbalance to the cool fall night. The soup was savory and salty with just a hint of sweetness from the onions and tartness from the cheese. She took another bite, then another. Soon she was scraping bread from the bottom of her trencher and wishing she had something to drink. She was just about to find water when she felt a thump beside her on the bench.

"I've been looking all over for you two," Sassy said. "I heard about Isolde. Rough break."

Something inside Emma relaxed when she heard Sassy's voice. She still felt awful about not being about to help Isolde, but it was good to have the gang back together. "I guess we were wrong about Ezell and Isolde being the same people."

"What can I say? Those are the breaks." Sassy put his front paws onto the table and leaned over Emma's empty trencher.

He sniffed it and made a face. "What do you say we get me one of those turkey legs I've seen people carrying around?"

"I'd have to get some more emerald tokens. You wouldn't believe how much they charge for a bowl of soup around here. But first, I'm dying to know what happened to you. Where have you been? Where's your parrot costume?"

Sassy hesitated for a fraction of a second before replying. "I had to ditch it."

"Why?"

"My cover got blown."

"How?"

"I came across a real parrot. He started asking me questions I couldn't answer. It's a shame really." Sassy arched his back, then sat on his haunches. "If I'd had time to research the part, maybe I wouldn't have been exposed."

Emma couldn't be sure, but Sassy seemed to be chuckling to himself. "What about Ezell? Did you find her?"

"It only took a few minutes. I found her backstage, approached her and tried to warn her, but she didn't understand."

"She's not a fairy. She's human."

"I figured that out when she took off her wing and handed it to her crony."

"I'll bet."

"The coronation went off without a hitch, but something about her smelled fishy—and not in a good way. I decided to tail her. There's about a hundred of them just like her."

"You know, as much as I've heard about the Fairykin, I'm not sure I've seen one."

"That's because they're not out here mingling. They've set up a kind of hive behind the palace. They've set up barricades so that there's only way in and out. That's watched over by guards."

"Are you serious?" Emma asked.

"As a heart attack. I saw a lady in a trench coat try to go

in. They stopped her, and she had to wait for a good ten minutes before they got permission to let her in. She came back out a minute later and looked pretty mad."

Emma's pulse quickened. "What color was the trench coat?"

"Tan."

"Did she have a purse?"

"A red one, yeah. Why?"

"That was Linda from the Cappotelli crime family. They run an operation out of the faire to smuggle magic objects in from the fae realm. They have a certain calling card, a coin, which we found on Isolde's body."

Sassy looked impressed. "You've been busy."

"That group you saw, all wearing fairy wings? They're called the Fairykin. They're a cult, and they're moving in on the Cappotellis' business. We just heard Linda trying to get the faire's owner to kick them out." Emma bit her lower lip and tried to think the situation through. Why would Linda visit the Fairykin? Did she approach them before visiting Griffin, offering to buy them out? To pay them to camp in some other ren faire? Why had she been rebuffed so quickly? Emma turned to Sassy. "Were you able to get a look inside their camp?"

"Of course. Barricades are useless against my superior feline wjles. I slipped through a crack in the defenses and wandered around the camp, pretending to be a poor, lost stray. Ezell had a big throne, where she sat and gave orders to the other people in fairy wings."

"How many?"

"About a hundred. They were busy too, setting up tables, decorations, that sort of thing. It looked like they were about to have a party."

"A party?" Emma grinned. "That sounds like fun. I think we should go."

CHAPTER 17
COOL

Emma walked ahead of her friends, out of the food court, through a large arched stone passageway, into a bustling cobblestone thoroughfare lined with brightly colored tents selling every good imaginable. Vendors sold costumes, sparkling purple elixirs in bottles, glow sticks, and face paint and imported jewelry. Light-up battle-axes flashed in a rainbow of color. Half a dozen shopkeepers barked into microphones, trying to lure passersby to stop, shop, and spend. From far off came the sound of a balloon sucking up helium from a tank, followed by the sound of a balloon popping.

Emma smiled to herself. The mix of sights and sounds and smells had unlocked a hidden feeling in her heart, a kind of gaping wonder which she'd felt as a kid wandering through the Oklahoma State Fair. Back then, as she wandered wide-eyed between carnival games with their enormous stuffed-animal prizes, it had seemed as though the normal world had been stripped away and replaced by something beautiful and glittering and just a little dangerous.

"Wait up, Emma!" Riley jogged to her side and matched

her pace. "You don't really plan on just walking up to the gate and crashing the Fairykin party, do you?"

"It's not crashing if you have an invitation." Emma waved the Fairykin pamphlet in the air like a golden ticket.

"You don't have an invitation. That's just a brochure they use to recruit people."

"Easy, then we'll be recruits." Emma slowed her pace slightly so she could examine each of the shops as they passed. It was only a hunch, but Emma felt certain that she'd find what she was looking for somewhere in this blinking monument to consumerism.

"It's one thing to show up at their meetings, where they expect new people. It's another to show up at their secret base, at night, during a party."

"If anything, that will make it easier for us. The Fairykin will be too busy celebrating their queen to pay much attention to a few newcomers. They won't know we're there."

"Aren't you forgetting that they all have fairy wings, and we don't? We'll stand out like sore thumbs."

"No." Emma stopped suddenly in front of one of the shops and smiled. "I didn't forget that. It's why I wanted to come here."

The shop in front of them was lit in sparkling neon pink. Along the back wall hung pair after pair of wings. There were large wings covered with sparkles and tiny black bat wings scalloped at the bottom. A Bluetooth speaker mounted over-head played a breathy pan-flute song. A bored teenager sat by the register reading an ancient paperback.

"No. It's not happening," Sassy said, padding up to them in no particular hurry.

Emma plastered on her most persuasive smile. "Come on, Sassy, you know you want to dress up like a fairy to sneak into the Fairykin party."

"Absolutely not. I've suffered enough indignity for one day, thank you very much. You two can disguise yourselves however you want. I'll make my way in. Or do I even need to bother? I'm a little fuzzy on our objectives here."

"Simple," Emma replied. "We find Ezell and question her about the murder."

Sassy laughed. "That simple, huh? And I imagine you have some magical elixir to make her tell the truth?"

Emma frowned. To be honest, she hadn't spent much time thinking about what would happen *after* she confronted Ezell. She just kind of assumed something would occur to her. It usually did. "Just leave that to me." She did her best to sound confident but fell short.

"While you're at it, you might want to come up with a plan to keep them from kicking you out once they realize you're only there to ambush Ezell."

"Since you seem to know so much, why don't you tell me your plan?" Emma asked.

"Eh? I don't have one."

"Not so easy, is it?"

"I'll tell you what," Sassy said. "I'll sneak in. I'll keep an eye on things. If you run into any trouble, just holler."

"That's a great plan. I'll feel better knowing you're out there."

"Just try not to get yourselves hurt. If the Fairykin killed Isolde, they're not going to be too happy about a couple of strangers asking questions." Sassy turned and walked away.

Emma watched Sassy disappear into the crowd. As much as she tried to pretend that she was on top of things, that her plan was foolproof, she knew deep down that it was a little crazy. But it was the only way forward. If she had to walk that path, she was glad to know that Sassy would be out there watching her, ready to jump in and protect her. She smiled.

"Um, were you just, like, talking to a cat?" The cashier asked in a monotone. She looked over the top of her paperback. Her head was cocked to the side, and she wore a puzzled expression.

"Yeah," Emma replied. "I was talking with a cat. It's okay. He talks back."

The corners of the cashier's mouth turned down into a frown, which she held for several silent seconds before shrugging. "First time I've seen that. Okay. Do you want some wings? We've got a 20 percent crazy-lady discount."

"I do want to buy some wings, yeah. For both of us," Emma said, gesturing to Riley.

"Cool, well, the discount is really for using cash instead of tokens. But I only offer it to crazy ladies."

"Why?"

"Not as likely to narc on me to the owner. When you use tokens, 20 percent goes to him."

"Ouch."

"Whatever. I just work here. But it's fun to cause a little chaos."

"I knew a chaos demon once," Emma said. "Believe it or not, he was a nice guy."

"You don't get a bigger discount for being crazier. You maxed that out already."

"It's a shame, because there's a lot more where that came from."

"What kind of wing experience are you wanting?" the cashier droned, not rising to the bait. "We have dragon wings, angel wings, bat wings, crow wings—"

"Just some ordinary, everyday fairy wings, thanks," Emma said. She saw quite a few pairs on the wall behind the cashier.

"Dark or light fairy?"

Emma paused. She hadn't known there were different kinds of fairy. "What's the difference?"

"One's dark and the other's light."

Emma glanced at Riley. "What do you think? Light? Okay, light. And make them extra sparkly."

"They come with sparkles."

"I know. It was just an expression."

"But we do offer an additional sparkle service for an additional twenty dollars each."

Emma shook her head. "The, ah, base model is fine."

"Wonderful. Just step over here and we'll get you fitted."

———

Emma and Riley stood in front of the wing store and examined each other. They both wore identical wings made of translucent white nylon stretched over a wire frame. A pattern made of imitation diamonds swirled and twisted on the fabric. The wings were held on to their backs by thin, clear plastic straps looped around their shoulders. They were just like the fairy wings that Emma had owned as a child, scaled up for an adult and drastically more expensive.

"You look good," Riley said.

"You do too. But I'm starting to wonder if it was a mistake to wear this coat during the fitting. Doesn't it seem a little weird that the wings are sprouting out of a pirate coat? Am I supposed to be Captain Hook or Tinker Bell?"

"I could say the same thing," Riley said, reaching around and adjusting the wings that seemed to spring out of their green Peter Pan tunic. "It's like an old episode of Star Trek where Pan and Hook and Tinker Bell get scrambled together in a transporter accident."

Emma looked at Riley blankly.

"Really? Not a Trekkie?"

"And that is?"

"You don't know what a Trekkie is? Have you seen Star Trek?"

"No?"

"Does Viv know about this?"

Emma shrugged. "I've got an overprotective mom. I never got a chance to watch a lot of shows back then."

"They had movies too."

"Well, I didn't get to watch those either."

"Okay," Riley said. "I'll tell you what we're going to do. As soon as we solve this mystery, we're going to go back to your place, grab Viv and Jessie, order a lot of snacks, and school you on the masterpiece that is Star Trek."

"Fine," Emma said. She felt a lump form in her throat. She didn't show it, but she always felt a little ashamed when people brought up movies or TV shows she didn't know. She swallowed and tried not to think about it. She had a killer to find, a dad to save, and a party to crash. "Sassy said the Fairykin camp is located behind the castle. Do you know where that is?"

"Yeah," Riley said. "It's not far from the stage where they had the coronation. It'll be empty now. We shouldn't have any trouble getting in this time."

"Let me guess. It's this way?" Emma pointed down a path that led away to their left.

"How did you know?"

"Elementary, my dear Riley." Emma opened her palm, revealing the magic compass. Its lid lay open. The arrow pointed left.

Riley laughed. "Cheater."

———

Emma and Riley walked down the main thoroughfare leading to the coronation stage. It was empty now, and they moved quickly across the cobblestones. What a difference a few hours made! The air was silent and still, nothing like the earlier crush of bodies. Emma noticed for the first time that trees overhung the paths, their branches wrapped in fairy lights. A crow, late to bed, cawed and leaped from a branch, taking flight.

The path led them to a large open area and an empty stage that loomed darkly behind steel crowd-control barriers.

"That must be the Fairykin camp." Riley pointed into the distance where light danced on Douglas fir crowns at the edge of the tree line where the faire ended and the forest began.

They walked toward the lights, past the dark stage and the empty backstage area. A small dirt trail led through a stand of trees. As they drew closer to the party, tree trunks became painted with shards of flashing light that filtered through the wood.

"Do you hear that?" Emma paused. She hadn't heard the sound so much as felt it deep in her stomach. It was a low thumping that beat in rhythm with the lights flashing on the trees. "I'd say we found our fairy party. To be honest, I expected something more old-fashioned, but this sounds like a rave."

The more they walked, the more detail they heard in the music. The low, thumping bass resolved into a hypnotic groove that slid up and down the scale to the electronic rhythm of a drum machine and a melody like an alarm clock.

"Okay." Emma turned to Riley. "We're going to go up to the gate. If it's not guarded, we'll slip in. Otherwise, we'll flash the pamphlet and say that one of the Fairykin gave it to us, and they invited us to the party tonight."

"What did they look like?" Riley asked.

"Who?"

"The Fairykin who invited us. In case they ask."

"Let's say it was a girl with brown hair and glasses." The trail narrowed. Shrubs and creeping vines pressed in from both sides. Emma swatted them away.

"Tall or short?"

"Tall."

"Did she have an accent?"

"What?"

"A regional accent?"

"No, she sounded like a local."

"How old was she?"

"Does it matter? Look, the music's going to be so loud they won't be able to hear us let alone give us the third degree." Even here, Emma had to raise her voice to be heard over the pulsing electronic dance music coming from somewhere ahead. She came to a stop. The trail had been narrowing for some time. Now it was a small dirt strip running through a tunnel of barren autumn foliage. Emma continued. "It probably won't come up. After all, we did buy these awesome fairy wings. And they'll probably be so busy with their party that they won't notice us." Emma pushed the branches away from her face and gulped. They were here.

To their right, Emma saw the silhouette of a castle. It was like an old movie set, where the buildings were all cutouts. It seemed likely to be painted on the front with stones and windows and turrets. From the rear, it looked like someone had patched a couple dozen sheets of plywood together and propped them up against a rickety lumber scaffold.

The space behind the castle was a large open, undeveloped area. If you were a fairy cult looking to set up a private encampment, you couldn't pick a better spot. The Fairykin had made it even more exclusive by dragging in barricades, boxes, and random pieces of scrap and piling them up into a large makeshift wall. Behind it, the music bumped and swayed.

"What was that you said about slipping in unnoticed?" Riley said, extending a finger and pointing at the long line of wingless fairgoers waiting by the entrance. At the head of the line, a bouncer let people in. He was a huge lumberjack of a man with bulging muscles, a red plaid shirt, and teensy-tiny fairy wings.

Emma grinned. "This is even better. We'll just get in line

with everyone else. Blend in." Emma walked to the back of the line as if she knew exactly what she was doing.

But the more she looked around, the more doubt assailed her. The people in line were, well, kids. None of them looked a day over twenty-five. Emma suddenly felt acutely aware of the fact that she knew who shot JR. She knew how to use a rotary phone. She remembered a time when you went to the mall to buy music and when you had to wait a week to see photos you just took.

Even worse, none of the people in line wore fairy wings. Sure, they wore costumes, but not in a way that suggested geekdom. They looked like they were backstage at Coachella, like they were partying at Burning Man. In a word, they looked cool.

No.

They looked like they'd make fun of her for saying *cool*, that tired, midcentury word. They would no doubt be using some infinitely newer, hotter, hipper slang.

Ahead, Emma saw a familiar face. The tall elf-eared teenager who'd been recording videos in the coronation crowd stood just in front of them. Emma tapped on his shoulder. "Excuse me."

"Huh?" He looked down at Emma and Riley like they were Martians just emergency landed in Times Square.

"Do you know what's going on here?"

"It's, uh, the Fairykin party? What are you doing here if you don't know that?"

"Just… trying to have a good time?" Emma cringed the moment she said it.

"Well, okay. You know they don't just let everybody in. You need a ticket." He flashed a small slip of paper embossed with gold lettering.

Great. They had actual tickets. There was no way she and Riley would be able to flash a brochure, show off their wings, and slip in. "Where can we get tickets?"

"Beats me." He shrugged and turned around.

There was no way he would brush them off like that. Emma tapped him again on his shoulder. "You must have gotten your ticket somewhere."

"Yeah, I got it somewhere."

"Would it hurt you to tell me where?"

"Some guy gave it to me. They wanted people with a certain vibe."

Emma glanced at the people in line. It was easy to tell what vibe they wanted. Young, bored, attractive. She wouldn't have made the cut even when she'd been in her early twenties. And now? There was no chance that she'd pass the vibe check. She appraised the kid in front of her. What did he want? What had she wanted when she was just out of college trying to carve out her place in life? Ahh yes. She remembered. Money.

"I want to buy your ticket," Emma said.

He looked at her in disbelief. "You want to… Do you like this kind of music? Shouldn't you be listening to Glen Miller or something?"

"How old do you think I am?"

"I don't know. Sixty?"

"Excuse me! Even if I *was* sixty, I'd be too young for Glen Miller. But to answer your question, I don't care about the music. There's somebody inside I need to talk to."

"Who?"

"Ezell."

"You're crazy."

"You're not the first person to call me crazy tonight. Now answer my question. How much?"

"I don't know. I'm not sure I want to sell my ticket. It looks like a rad party."

"Everybody has a number. How much?"

"Uh…" He stared into the distance for a moment. "Five hundred?"

"Dollars?" Emma had to stop herself from shouting. "You want me to pay five hundred dollars for a single ticket?"

"It says you can bring a plus one," he offered helpfully, "so you and your friend could go together."

Emma sighed. Not only did she remember how to use a rotary phone, but she also remembered when you could get into an arena concert for fifty bucks. Now this kid wanted five hundred for a ticket to a party she'd probably get kicked out of for not being cool enough. Five hundred bucks was just about all she had left of the money Vanessa had paid her earlier. But she had to solve this case, and to do that, she needed to confront Ezell. Emma gritted her teeth and reached for her wallet. "I'll give you four hundred cash."

The kid sighed and looked at the ticket like he was trying to make a hard decision. But his mouth quivered as he tried to keep from grinning. "It's a deal."

Emma counted out four of Linda's crisp hundreds and exchanged them for the ticket. She was surprised at how luxurious it felt. The soft cream-colored paper was foiled with gold and embossed with ornate lettering that read: THIS TICKET ALLOWS THE BEARER AND ONE GUEST TO ENTER THE EXCLUSIVE CORONATION PARTY OF EZELL FAIRYKIN.

"Thanks," Emma said, but the kid was already walking away, stuffing the money in his jeans.

"That was surprisingly easy," Riley said.

"For you, maybe, but that was the last of my money." Doubt poked at the back of Emma's mind. The kid looked awfully happy. Had she paid too much? Probably, but they didn't have time to waste negotiating the finer points. She had to get inside that party because Ezell was there. And Ezell could be the key to busting this case wide open.

At least the line moved quickly. You probably didn't need a bouncer when the guests were preselected. Still, as they approached the hulking man, Emma felt a lump form in her throat. What if he didn't let them in?

"All right," the man said in a rumbly voice. He was speaking to the couple at the front of the line. Even though they didn't wear fairy wings, they were so thin and precious-looking that Emma wouldn't have been surprised if they'd sprouted them there and then. "Your tickets look in good order. Go on. Now, what do we have here?" He looked Emma and Riley up and down. "Do you have a ticket?"

"We do."

The bouncer seemed surprised. He took their ticket and eyed it suspiciously. He rubbed the ticket between his thumb and forefinger, apparently testing some quality of the paper. He lifted it to his nose and sniffed it. "Genuine," he muttered to himself before looking back at Emma. "Where did you find this?"

CHAPTER 18
BLACK AND WHITE

The bouncer, a mountain of a man dressed in plaid with tiny, sparkly fairy wings, stared at Emma, waiting for a reply. Emma's pulse quickened. She felt the weight of the line behind her. Everyone looking at her, judging her, wishing she'd get out of the way. An electric shock ran through her body. It told her to move, to run, to get out of there, but the bouncer's gaze pinned her like a moth. The way he looked at her said he knew she didn't belong. The words he'd spoken drove the last nail in the coffin. Where had she found the ticket?

Found the ticket.

Not acquired, not accepted, but *found.* He must have thought a real invitee had dropped it and Emma, desperate middle-aged woman that she was, scooped it up to present as her own.

None of that mattered, Emma tried to remind herself. None of these opinions mattered. Her own discomfort didn't even matter. No, the only thing that mattered now was finding Isolde's killer. If that meant looking like a cougar trying to crash a rave, so be it.

"I didn't find the ticket." Emma surprised even herself

with how confident she sounded. "Someone gave it to us. They said we passed the vibe check."

"Who?"

"They didn't tell me their name. It was a girl… with brown hair and glasses."

The bouncer squinted down at Emma. "Was she tall or short?"

"Tall."

"Did she have an accent?"

"What?"

"A regional accent?"

"No, she sounded like a local."

"How old was she?"

"What's this? An interrogation? Are you going to let us in or not?"

The bouncer stepped back. He apparently hadn't counted on Emma to come out swinging. He stared at her for a heartbeat, confusion written on his face, then shrugged and waved them in. "Fine, go. They're not paying me enough to care."

Emma and Riley barely made it through the gate before they burst out laughing.

"I told you we should have figured out how old they were!" Riley shouted over the booming dance music.

"We got in, didn't we? Who knows? If I'd answered the question, I might have been wrong."

"I just didn't expect you to go full can-I-speak-with-your-manager. It's kind of a superpower."

"I promise to use it for good!"

"What?" Riley cupped their hand to their ear.

"I said, I promise to use it for good!" Emma shouted. She looked around and smiled, feeling the tension drain from her body. It didn't matter that the music was loud enough to make her ears ring. It didn't matter that she was older than everyone here. She'd been quick on her feet and gotten them through the gate.

The Fairykin camp was smaller than it appeared from the outside. It was ringed all around by the same type of scrap-wood barricade that walled off the front. Guests streamed in the gate behind them, into space about the size of a roller rink. At the far end, a DJ with pink gelled hair held a head-phone against his ear with one hand and adjusted knobs with the other. The song that was playing faded, merging into another song with the same hypnotic tempo.

Someone pushed around them, jostling Emma. She caught a whiff of body odor and other even more pungent smells. This party was like most of the parties she'd been to. It looked better from the outside.

Suddenly the music stopped. The DJ handed his micro-phone to a man dressed like a court jester. He wore a full-body green-and-white-checkered leotard made of stretchy material, along with a jester's hat. From the distance that Emma stood, it looked like he wore a velvet octopus on his head, only it had six legs, each of which was tipped with a bell. He jingled as he took the stage.

"Greetings and salutations!" the jester said. "Salutations and greetings! Fairykin and Fairy. King and pauper. Lion and lamb, welcome all. Tonight, we feast, we frolic, we f— We celebrate the crowning of our queen!"

Cheers went up. The crowd was a fifty-fifty mix of those with wings and those without. The wing wearers let out full-throated cheers. They clapped and hooted. They were obvi-ously Fairykin. Those without wings varied. Some were enthusiastic. Some seemed confused. Emma guessed that they'd been invited as possible recruits.

"Can I get a round of boisterous applause for our very own DJ Funky Times!" The jester waited for the applause to die down. "In a moment, I will introduce our queen, our belle of the ball to the ball of the belle and the party will commence in earnest. But for now, I have a single question for you to answer."

Silence blanketed the crowd, followed shortly by nervous laughter. Someone coughed. But the jester stood and stared blankly at the crowd as if waiting. Eventually someone yelled, "What's the question?"

"I'm so glad you asked! I would like you to tell me why I brought this pencil to the party today." The jester held a pencil in front of him at arm's length.

Silence descended once more. People seemed too confused to even whisper.

"I brought it, of course, to *draw* a crowd!" The DJ pressed a button, and a rim shot played over the speakers.

The crowd groaned. Was this guy really going to do a standup-comedy routine? Sure, he was dressed like a jester, but did he really take it that literally?

"Didn't like that one, huh? But do you have any idea what would happen if you held a ren faire without jesters? Why, it'd be a *faire-ly* serious mistake." Rim shot.

Someone booed, and suddenly a whole chorus of boos rose from the crowd.

"That's just mean!" the jester said. "Okay, I get it, folks. I really do. You're not a fan of modern comedy served up in new and unexpected ways. No, you want solid fare. Meat and potatoes. Real, stick-to-your-ribs material. I understand! In fact, I'm something of a traditionalist myself. Therefore, for my last number, let me ask you a question that's beguiled philosophers throughout the centuries. A riddle that plunges into the heart of existence itself. A conundrum that—"

"Hurry up!" someone shouted.

"Fine." The jester brought his hand to his heart to show how hurt he felt by the outburst. "Why did the chicken cross the playground?"

Once again, the crowd went silent, but this time you could have cut the tension with a knife.

"To get to the other slide." The jester ducked, narrowly avoiding a trencher of soup that someone had thrown at him.

"Thank you. You've been a lovely crowd. I'd tell you to tip your waitstaff, but we don't have any. And now, without any further ado, I give you your Emerald Queen Ezell!"

The DJ played a processional full of trumpet and drum and fife. Then a woman in an emerald dress and crown took the stage. She wore an enormous pair of translucent wings that made Emma's look like the cheap toys they were. She took the microphone and began thanking the audience, but Emma was too preoccupied to notice what she said.

Emma turned to Riley. "Looks like we found her."

"Now what do we do?"

But before Emma could answer, horns sounded and the dance party began in earnest. She'd thought the music was loud before, but now she realized it had only been light background music played while the guests were arriving.

The bass was so thick it rattled her teeth. It wrenched her stomach and blurred her vision. The high notes were even worse, stabbing at her eardrums until they felt like they were going to bleed. Then came the lights, flashing pulsars of red and white and green pointed directly at the audience. Were parties always this bright? This loud? Everyone in the ren faire had to be able to hear it. If the Fairykin ever hoped to keep their camp a secret from the authorities, they'd blown it.

Emma looked at Riley and raised her shoulders in the universal gesture of "I don't know what to do." She and Riley might as well have been on separate planets. Maybe they could text each other? Emma reached to take out her phone, but her gaze fell onto the stage and her stomach sank.

Ezell, the Emerald Queen, was gone. She wasn't in the crowd in front of the stage either. Her sparkly wings and bright green dress would have been easy to spot in the flashing light. Emma did see someone she recognized though. The jester came forward from the back of the stage, took off his hat, and jumped down to crowd level. He made a beeline for a spot in the enclosing wall just behind and to the left of the stage. He slipped through.

Emma tapped Riley on the shoulder and pointed to the gap. They set off together and arrived a few moments later. They approached the gap in the wall cautiously. But if there had been a guard, they had obviously abandoned their post the minute the dancing started. Emma slipped through.

It was dark out of the glare of the flashing lights. Though the music was still present, it wasn't nearly so loud behind the speakers. Emma looked around, trying to orient herself. They were alone.

The space behind the camp seemed to serve as storage, staging area, and junkyard all at once. Piles of leftover scrap wood from the walls littered the ground. To their right, heavy-duty black-and-chrome flight cases were neatly stacked, ready to protect the speaker system, lights, and turntables on the ride back to whatever trendy converted loft space DJ Funky Times called home.

Ahead of them, light spilled out of the windows of a parked Winnebago RV. It was painted '90s beige. Even in the low light, Emma could see rust spotting the chrome trim. The chassis shifted, and voices could be heard through the RV's thin walls.

"I told you, Brad, I don't feel like dancing. Did you see them? They don't care about me. They just came for the party."

"How can we recruit them to the cause if they're just partying with their friends?" a man, probably Brad, replied.

"You should have thought of that before coming up with this plan!"

"Come, children, don't fight." A third voice broke in. It sounded familiar, but Emma had the hardest time placing it, until she suddenly realized it was the jester's voice stripped of all its mirth. It had a slippery, slithering quality that gave Emma chills. "Recruitment isn't our only goal. Whatever brings us popularity increases our power and furthers our aims. As such, the figure of the queen is quite important."

Ezell sighed. "Do you have any idea how much work it is to walk around all day in a princess dress with heels?" She didn't wait for a response. "Fine. Give me twenty minutes and I'll go back out there. Until then, I'm on break."

"Twenty minutes," the jester said.

The RV shifted again. Someone inside was moving. A jolt of fear ran up Emma's back. She turned to Riley. "Let's hide."

"Agreed," Riley said, looking around for a hiding spot. They pointed to the stack of flight cases.

Emma nodded, and they hid behind the cases. A few moments later, the RV door opened and the jester walked out, followed by a boring-looking man with a beard, probably Brad. They strolled toward the gap in the wall.

"Are you sure she's committed?" the jester asked. "After what our… friend said yesterday, I have my doubts."

"Positive," Brad said.

"We have a lot riding on this year's faire. We've made our play. If it doesn't pay out, we'll be exposed for fools."

"You're one to talk."

The jester laughed. "The beautiful thing about the fool is that he can speak plainly. He can announce that the king is a bore, the queen is a chore, and the prince is soft in the head. In a word, the fool is the only one allowed to tell the truth."

"Is that what you did with that Cappotelli woman? Tell the truth?"

"Quiet, you fool," the jester said, his eyes darting left and right. "Names have power."

"Don't tell me you believe all that hocus-pocus mumbo jumbo."

"I believe in a world that's not so black-and-white as the one which you apparently inhabit. And in my world, there are many kinds of truth, some of which are not strictly factual." The jester slipped through the gap in the wall, followed by Brad.

"Now's our chance!" Emma said, heart pounding. "She's in the trailer alone."

"I wonder what they meant by 'making their play,'" Riley said.

"Maybe Ezell will tell us," Emma said over her shoulder as she walked up to the RV and knocked.

An annoyed voice came from the other side of the door. "Listen, Brad, I told you I was taking a break! I've been running my buns off since the sun came up, and I'm not going to dance right now." The door swung open to reveal Ezell in her green dress and bare feet. She glanced between Emma and Riley, apparently trying to make sense of the two strangers. "You know the party's over there, right?"

"We know," Emma said.

"Okay…" She stretched the word out. "I'm not going to give you my autograph or anything."

"We want to talk with you about Isolde."

The name set her back on her heels, but she recovered quickly. "I suppose you'd better come in."

Emma climbed two steps and found herself in a narrow aisle. To her left were the driver's and passengers' seats. To the right, a seating area, then a kitchen farther back. All of it had the dingy look of plastic that had once been cream-colored but had darkened and yellowed with age. The air smelled faintly of mildew and stale beer.

"Have a seat." Isolde gestured at a deep bench topped with pastel pink cushions. "I'd offer you some refreshments, but we don't have any."

"It's okay," Emma said, sitting down. Despite its fluffy appearance, the bench cushion must have been mostly air. It deflated as soon as she sat on it and left her basically sitting on hard plastic. Emma's tailbone cried out in protest, but she forced herself to ignore it.

"I just heard about Isolde," Ezell said. "They told me she's dead. It seems unbelievable."

"Oh, it's real," Emma said. "We were there when they found her."

"What happened?"

"Murder."

Ezell's mouth hung open slightly, and she stared vacantly into space. She came to her senses. "I didn't know it was even possible for her kind to die. You know that she was…"

"A fairy, yeah."

"She was so much more than that. She was the first real-life fairy I ever met. She was the reason I bought my first pair of wings. She was the reason I started the Fairykin."

"What do you mean?"

"Didn't you pay attention during your orientation?" She glanced at Emma. Her gaze fell onto Emma's wings and her eyes narrowed. "Wait a minute, those aren't Fairykin wings. They look like the cheap knockoffs they sell out front. Who are you?"

"We're working on behalf of Isolde's's family."

"You mean… the Fairy Kingdom?"

"The what? No. Let's just say the people we work for are more distant relatives. They knew she was in danger, and they sent us."

"To save her?"

"To find her killer."

"Oh." Ezell shrank. The stark truth seemed to punch a hole in her ideas about the Fairy Kingdom. "I guess I'd better help you then. What do you need to know?"

"Why don't you start by answering my question? Why did you start the Fairykin?"

"Okay, but first you have to tell me something. Did you know Isolde?"

"No."

"That's a shame. I can tell you the story, but to really

understand it, you have to know her." Ezell looked out of the window and sighed. "It happened six years ago. I was in pretty rough shape. My husband had just run off with my best friend. I was depressed, couldn't make myself get out of bed for work, so they fired me. I fell behind on rent and was a hairbreadth away from eviction. That's when I saw her walking past my apartment."

"You saw Isolde?"

"She was the most beautiful person I'd ever seen. It was a dreary, rainy day, but she had her own light. She glowed." Even now, so many years later, the memory seemed to choke Ezell up. "She was everything I wasn't and wanted to be. Just seeing her made me feel whole again. So I did something kind of crazy. I threw on my raincoat, rushed out the door, and followed her."

"You tailed her?"

"I told you it was crazy. I hadn't dressed for the cold, and I was freezing, but I couldn't stand the thought of losing her. We must have walked for about an hour. Eventually, we wound up here." She raised her arms in a gesture that included the whole faire. "That's when I saw something that changed me forever. She had been wearing a kind of bulky coat. But once she stepped into the faire, she took it off and she had wings!"

"Did you know she was a fairy?"

"I didn't care. I just wanted to be her. I didn't bring my wallet, so I couldn't buy a ticket and follow her inside. But the next day I came back. I used the last bit of money in my account to buy a cheap pair of wings, and the rest was history. Isolde didn't know it, but she saved my life. She saved a lot of people's lives."

Emma stared at Ezell and wondered how much of her story was true. It felt bizarre, unhinged. But people did crazy things when they were at rock bottom. They found hope in the unlikeliest places. Ezell seemed sincere enough, but her story didn't line up with the deputy assistant warden's. "You seem to care a great deal for Isolde."

"I do."

"I've heard that you two were fighting yesterday. Voices were raised."

Ezell's cheeks flushed red. "Who told you that? It was a private conversation."

"Any number of people might have heard the yelling," Emma said. "What were you fighting about?"

"Like I told you, it was private."

"Surely any claim to privacy that Isolde might have had vanished when she was murdered? Whatever you were talking about might be the key to finding her killer."

"It had nothing to do with her murder."

"You can't know that," Emma said. "And I'm sure you can see how suspicious it looks for—"

"Suspicious? You think *I* could have killed Isolde? She meant everything to me!" Ezell stood, looking like she didn't know whether to storm out or send Emma and Riley packing.

Emma's heart raced. If she alienated Ezell now, she'd lose a valuable source of information. "I'm sorry. I'll stop asking about it."

"Fine," Ezell said, crossing her arms.

"Maybe instead, you could tell me how you know Linda Cappotelli."

When she heard the name, the color drained from Ezell's face. She sat and sank into the bench like she wished she could disappear. When she looked up, all traces of the bubbly Fairykin Emerald Queen were gone. Her eyes were hard and her voice low and filled with malice. "Linda Cappotelli killed Isolde."

CHAPTER 19
FOUND

Silence hung thick between Emma, Riley, and Ezell. The only sound in the muggy, musty RV was the muted thumping of dance music bleeding through its thin walls. The music was a heartbeat drumming faster and louder. The light show pulsed quicker and brighter to the tempo of the music, flashing through the RV windows. It cast crossbar shadows on the opposite wall.

Linda Cappotelli killed Isolde.

It wasn't as though the possibility never occurred to Emma. The Caligula coin on Isolde's lips made Linda a prime suspect. But to hear it spoken aloud, to have the weight of those words hang in the musty air, to share them like a secret with Riley and Ezell made the situation seem suddenly, overwhelmingly, real.

"How do you know?" Emma heard herself say. "What evidence do you have?"

"Evidence?" Ezell scoffed. "It's obvious. She was going to end her relationship with the Cappotellis. I convinced her to talk with her people about breaking it off."

"Why?"

"The Cappotellis are mobsters. Criminals. Have you seen *The Grandfather*?"

Emma glanced quickly to Riley, then back to Ezell. "You're the second person to ask me that today."

"They're taking advantage of the fairies. Trading them DVDs of garbage TV shows for priceless magical artifacts."

Emma remembered what Merlin had told her. Creatures like fairies and the fae can't create. They have no arts or music of their own. They're willing to pay almost any price for the products of human creativity. Ezell didn't know that. "Did the fairies think it was a fair deal?"

Ezell let out a frustrated sigh. "They're not from this plane of existence. They don't cheat or steal. They're better than us in every way, but they're like children, defenseless."

"You wanted to protect them from the Cappotellis?"

"Is that so wrong? I've been trying to make them see reason for years. It was like beating my head against the wall. Finally though, something shifted in Isolde. I don't know why, but I could sense it. She started listening to me. Agreeing with me."

"But you still fought."

"I told you that's private."

"What about your conversation with Linda Cappotelli? Is that private too?"

"She accused me of edging in on her turf. She thought I tried to convince the fairies to trade with the Fairykin instead of with her, uh, organization."

"You're not?"

"No! I want to free the fairies, not exploit them!" Whatever someone might think about Ezell, this was real emotion.

"What about the rest of the Fairykin?"

Ezell hesitated for a moment before answering. "I am the queen. I started the Fairykin. I run the meetings. I bring new members into the fold."

"What about the other two, the jester and what's his

name? Brad? We saw them practically order you to leave the RV and go to the dance."

Ezell's lips drew back into a thin line. Her eyes became hard. "I am the queen."

"But they were at the meeting with Linda. What was their role?"

"I don't know what you're talking about. I met with her alone."

"Did Linda make you any offers?"

"You mean the money? I don't care about money. All I care about is my relationship with Isolde and the other fairies. If Isolde stays here, I'm staying here. And where I go, the Fairykin go."

"Did you say those words to Linda?"

"Why does it matter?"

"Just tell me."

"Yes, I told her exactly that. I don't see what any of this has to do with finding the murderer."

"Did she threaten you when you refused the money?"

"Not exactly. Maybe? Said something about bringing the whole thing crashing down. She had receipts. She knew where to look. I didn't know what she meant. I tried to tell her that she was focusing on the wrong things, that if she'd open her heart to the fairies, she wouldn't have to be so angry all the time. But she laughed at me and stormed off."

"Where did she go?"

"Away? I don't know!" She reached into a bag and checked her phone. "Look, I've got to go."

"Because the jester told you to?"

"Because the Fairykin want to see their queen."

———

Emma and Riley walked along a narrow path surrounded by trees. The party was far behind them and the cool air pricked

Emma's nose and cheeks. Emma's ears still rang from the thunderous music, but every step took her closer to quiet, peace, and relaxation. She felt the tension drain from her body, but her mind raced.

She'd gone into her interview with Ezell expecting to find a cynical, hard-nosed woman using her culty influence to further her goals and increase her wealth. What she'd found had left her feeling, well, sad.

Say what you want about the Fairykin, about their silly costumes and misplaced veneration. Their queen was a true believer. Emma didn't doubt the truth of her following Isolde and finding a strange sort of salvation. To her, fairies were the embodiment of light and good and happiness and everything else she wished she could be but wasn't.

Emma had never met a living fairy, but she had her doubts. They might not be dangerous like the fae, but they were related. That alone made Emma hesitant to trust them. The fae had put her family through hell. It made Emma feel sick to her stomach.

"Penny for your thoughts?" Riley said.

Emma flashed a wry smile. "How about an ancient Roman coin?"

"Price has gone up."

"Inflation." Emma chuckled mirthlessly. "I kind of feel bad for Ezell."

"I know, right?" Riley said.

"Something's shady with those other two. The jester and Brad. They have a hold on her. Did you hear the way they bossed her around?"

"And the way they spoke about her in private. I wonder what they meant when they talked about making their move."

"They have their own agenda, that's for sure. I don't think for a second they joined the Fairykin to commune with divine creatures of laughter and light." Emma bit her lower lip. "Did you notice the thing about Linda Cappotelli?"

"No, what?"

"We overheard Brad mention that they met with her. Remember? He asked the jester if he told her the truth, and the jester made up some nonsense about there being different kinds of truth."

"Oh yeah!" Riley said, mimicking the jester's accent. "Some types of truth are not so factual. What a douche."

Riley was right. Those guys seemed like grade A jerks. Emma wished she could wave a wand and make them disappear from Ezell's life. She'd probably be happier. But that wasn't her point. "They talked about meeting Linda Cappotelli. But Ezell said they didn't attend the meeting."

"Yeah, she seemed kind of sensitive about it. Is she covering for them? Maybe they said something or did something at the meeting that would incriminate the Fairykin?"

"There's one way to find out."

"How?"

"We'll find Linda and ask her. After all, we have a magic compass." Emma reached into her breast pocket and pulled out Merlin's compass. The smooth metal felt warm in her hand. She slipped her fingernail under its cover and popped it open. "If this works as well as it has been, Linda should be due east of here."

"That's your plan? Approach the Mafia heiress and ask her point-blank about her business?"

"Why not? She needs me to contact her father's spirit. Without me, she'll never find his will. She won't inherit. And besides, it will give me a chance to return her stupid priceless coin."

"Which one?"

"Both of them!"

It didn't take long for the evening chill to cool the metal compass in Emma's hand, to turn it into an icy weight that grew heavier with every step. It led them east, along the narrow, wooded trail, then south into a main thoroughfare. The compass seemed to know not only its destination but also the pathways coursing through the fairgrounds. It changed direction at each forking path like a mute, magical GPS.

It was getting late, and the faire was winding down. They passed a bearded bard in satin pants tucking his lute into a formfitting black plastic case. Next to him, a row of carnival games shut off its lights as its workers locked it up for the night. The rest of the fairgoers stumbled, bleary from turkey and ale, toward the exits.

"Where's the compass taking us?" Emma said.

"Hard to say, though it appears that we're generally moving toward the coronation stage." As if in response to Riley's words, the compass veered left, taking them through a small gap in a plywood barricade and onto the staff access road where they'd met Griffin a lifetime ago.

Generators hummed, powering the portable lampposts. Last time they'd been here, it had still been light enough to see without them. Now the sky around the bright halogen lights might as well have been made of the blackest black velvet. Emma shrank. It gave her the feeling of being on stage, watched, under interrogation. Unconsciously, she picked up her pace.

A moment later, they walked through a familiar gate into a large open space without any electric light. The only light came from the moon and stars above. It sketched the barest outline of a tree in the distance.

"Riley," Emma said, reaching into her purse for the flashlight she always carried. "We asked the compass to take us to Linda Cappotelli. Why did it bring us back to the world tree?"

"Are you sure that we asked? Technically, we just said we needed to find her."

"That's all we did last time, and it took us to the Fairykin camp. And before that, when it took us to Griffin's office, we didn't exactly fill out a formal request."

"Maybe it's getting tired."

"The compass. Is getting tired."

"It sounds farfetched, but it is a magical compass, after all. The very idea of it is farfetched. None of us knows what powers it has or what set of rules it follows."

Emma had to admit Riley was right. When nothing made sense, anything could make sense. She flicked on the flashlight. She checked the compass. It pointed dead ahead. The flashlight cast a bright circle onto the ground which broadened into a long oval as it skated along the grass toward the world tree. "We've followed it this far. I guess there's no harm in going on."

She pulled her flashlight beam off the world tree. It brushed the gaping hole where the empty time capsule probably still sat and rushed back across the grass to Emma's feet where it illuminated an unexpected flash of pink.

"That's odd." Emma kept her flashlight trained on the pink thing and approached hesitantly. She knelt. It was a tube of lipstick, an expensive brand. It was half-submerged in a small puddle where water had collected in a long, straight furrow pressed into the ground. She picked the tube up and opened it. It was dry and clean inside, a tasteful neutral pink. A feeling of dread filled her stomach.

There were many ordinary reasons that a tube of lipstick might have fallen to the ground, especially in a public venue like the faire. But this wasn't a heavily trafficked area. As far as Emma could tell, it didn't seem to be in use. The only people she'd seen here had been the deputy assistant warden and his crew of two workmen.

Emma swallowed the lump in her throat and walked

toward the pit. She scanned her flashlight along the grass and soon found something glinting in the grass. It was a small silver powder compact. It lay half open, its beige powder cake broken and flaking out around it. Her flashlight must have caught the compact mirror and been reflected.

A few steps more and she felt her heart jump into her throat. There, on the grass, was a cherry-red leather purse. It was open, and its contents lay scattered. She'd seen this purse twice today, first in the morning in her living room. Next in the evening in front of Mr. Griffin's office. It was Linda Cappotelli's purse. With a growing sense of dread, it dawned on Emma why the compass had led her to the world tree and the dark pit in front of it.

She took the last few steps quickly, like bitter medicine. She shined her flashlight into the hole. Even though she knew what to expect, it still shocked her.

Linda Cappotelli had been given none of the care that Isolde had received. She wasn't beautifully arranged inside the concrete casket with her hands crossed over her chest, looking so alive she might wake up at any moment. Linda's body hadn't been placed at all. It was dumped.

She lay sprawled sideways across the open concrete box. Her head dangled back in a way that would convince even the most ardent optimist that the spirit had left the body. Her legs dangled backward off the box's other side. This had the unfortunate effect of thrusting her torso upward, making it easy to see the dagger plunged into her heart.

Nausea overwhelmed Emma. Her vision went blurry. She stepped back from the pit and dropped her flashlight. Its beam rolled, then settled, illuminating the world tree from below but leaving the rest of the scene, especially the pit, in horrible darkness.

"She's dead," Emma found herself saying. Her voice sounded strange, distant. "Whoever killed Isolde must have —" She stopped. Until this moment, she would have bet money that Linda had killed Isolde. All the evidence pointed that way. First, they had the coin. The Cappotelli trademark. Then they had Ezell's claim that she'd turned Isolde against the Cappotellis. Finally, there was the reputation of that family for, uh, murdering people.

Emma saw Riley pick up the flashlight, walk back to the pit, and shine the beam in. They were silent for a moment, walking around the top of the hole, apparently to get a better view of something. A moment later, Riley looked up. "I suppose there's not much question about the cause of death."

"Do you think?"

"Did you see the dagger?"

"The one in her chest?"

"Did you see the handle?"

"No."

"It's inlaid with green gemstones. Emeralds? They're laid out in a kind of triangle pattern. It just... struck me as being odd."

"It does sound weird," Emma said. A realization was dawning in her. "This isn't our crime to solve."

"What do you mean?"

"There's a big difference between a fairy and a human, at least as far as the police are concerned. Linda's body isn't going to conveniently disappear." Emma thought of Detective Sprott Stromberg, that horrible deputy who recently set up shop in Undertown. The faire wouldn't be in his jurisdiction, but if the cops here were anything like him, she wanted to stay as far away as possible. A police investigation would only slow her down, making it even harder for her to find Isolde's killer and rescue her dad from the fae realm. If she hadn't left her footprints and fingerprints all over the crime scene, she'd be tempted to walk away and let someone else discover the body.

And that was before she started considering the Mafia aspects of the situation.

But then, on the other hand, Riley was right. Whoever killed Isolde was likely to have killed Linda. It wasn't her case, but it related. Emma walked up to the edge of the pit, steeled herself, and looked in.

The first thing that struck her about the dagger was its size. It was larger than a chef's knife but shorter than a sword. It was made of metal the color of unpolished silver, and the handle was inlaid in green stones in a triangular pattern that reminded Emma of harlequins. It was, without a doubt, an absurd weapon to kill anyone with, let alone a Mafia heiress. "I wish I knew what it meant."

Another voice behind them replied. "Why don't you ask?"

Emma turned to see Sassy padding up to them. "There you are! I thought you were going to keep to the shadows and rescue us."

"It didn't look like you needed rescuing," Sassy said.

"I'll bet you were off trying to get one of those turkey legs," Emma said.

"I resent that. But seriously, why don't you summon Linda's spirit and ask her?"

"I guess I could try. Hold on." Emma closed her eyes and felt her body. She felt the weight of her coat on her shoulders. She felt the pressure at the waistline of her pants. She breathed in and out and sank into her power center. The world around her fell away. The cool evening air and the darkness vanished. The deeper she dove, the more she saw the slender silken threads that connected her to everyone living and everyone dead. She reached out with her mind and felt for any connections leading to Linda's body.

Nothing. Nada. Zilch. Linda's spirit was nowhere to be found. It was disappointing but not surprising. The recently dead usually took a while to pull themselves together after the initial shock of it. Emma shook her head. "She's gone."

"A shame," Sassy said.

"So where were you? I don't believe for a second that you've been shadowing us this whole time."

"I did for a while. Followed you in through the woods, past the guard, and backstage. I watched you hide from those creeps and go into that big van."

"It's called an RV."

"It seemed unlikely that you two would be in danger, so I followed the two men back into the party to eavesdrop on their conversation."

Emma turned to Sassy. "What did you hear?"

"You mean besides that noise you people call music? Not much, just a name."

"What name?"

"Merlin. Mean anything to you?"

CHAPTER 20
THIEF!

Emma and Riley let themselves into Merlin's tent. Sassy kept watch outside. It had only been a few days since they were there, but already some of the mounds of junk seemed to be in different places. The air was still overwhelmingly warm from the wood stove in the center of the room, although it had become quite a bit more humid and smelled like frying onions. Emma heard sizzling from the back of the tent. It was punctuated by a loud crash and then a thunderclap of a curse that faded into low rumbles, then complete silence.

"I say, who goes there? I tell you, young people have no respect, barging in at all hours, not bothering to knock." The wizard emerged from the back. He was wearing a pink frilly apron over his gray robes and scarves. He still had his wizard hat on, but the front bill was folded back and tied with a little string, possibly for better visibility while cooking.

Despite the overwhelming seriousness of the situation, Emma couldn't help but stifle a laugh. "Aren't you running a place of business here? I would think you'd appreciate the foot traffic."

"A place of…" Merlin looked around as if he'd never seen the mounds of junk or the roaring stove or the ancient, comfy armchairs. "Why I suppose I am running a shop, yes. But there is such a thing as operating hours, my girl. I was just about to tuck into a delightful steak-and-kidney pie. Come back tomorrow!"

"It can't wait!"

"Can't wait? Can't wait? Who do you think you are to tell me what can and cannot wait? What is your name, child?"

"Are you serious?"

"I'm always serious."

"You don't remember me?"

"It would be easier to remember you if you told me who you are."

"I was just in here a couple of hours ago. You gave me this!" Emma pulled out the magic compass and held it up for Merlin to see.

He swiped it from her hand, turned it, opened the lid, and squinted at the needle. He looked up with a suspicious expression. "This is mine. Where did you get this?"

"You gave it to me!"

"Preposterous!" He tucked the compass between his scarves. "Why, I should call the authorities in on you if it wasn't suppertime."

"Don't you remember anything? My name is Emma. This is Riley. We visited earlier today with Orion."

"Orion you say? Strange fellow. I'm sure I would have remembered if I saw him today. What day is it?"

"Saturday. We were trying to solve the murder of a fairy named Isolde. Ring any bells?"

"Isolde? A fairy, you say?" The wizard munched on his beard and stared into the distance. "That does sound familiar. Are you sure it was today? I seem to recall an Isolde, but that must have been years ago."

"It was today."

"No, no. I remember it quite clearly now. A certain coin was placed in her ear? No, that's not right. In her nose?"

"On her lips."

"Ah, yes! Her lips!"

"And this is the coin." Emma held the small coin between her thumb and forefinger. It caught the light and glinted yellow gold.

"Quite surprising it's still around all these years after Isolde passed. I imagine some collector would have—"

"Will you please stop talking and listen to me!" Emma's cheeks were hot and her heart pounded. She didn't have time for Merlin's scatterbrained replies. "Isolde was killed recently. I found her body today. I took this coin off her lips. We came here afterward to ask if you knew anything about it. You said it was enchanted and gave us your compass."

"For free?"

"Yes."

"That doesn't sound like something I would do. But I must admit what you're saying does ring a bell. You'll have to excuse me, but time can be so difficult when you're living multiple lives at once."

"I don't want to know what that means."

"Sometimes I wonder myself. Let me see the coin." Emma gave it to him. He held it up to the light, then brought it closer to his eye as if inspecting for pinholes. After a moment, he stopped that line of investigation and touched the coin to the tip of his tongue. "Cardamom! I remember perfectly now. Isn't it fascinating how taste and scent are linked to memory?"

"I'm sure it is, but we're kind of in a hurry."

"How can I help you?"

"I need to ask you a question. I thought it was a simple one, but now I'm not so sure. If I asked you about something that happened today, or maybe yesterday, could you answer?"

"Could I? I might be slightly unstuck in time, but I'm not the doting old fool you seem to think I am. Ask your question."

"Have you seen a jester?"

"Really! I thought you were going to ask me a hard question, like what I ate for breakfast. But no, you went to all this trouble, interrupted my dinner, implied that I'm senile only to ask me if I've seen a jester?"

"If it's an easy question, answer it."

"Yes."

"Excuse me?"

"Yes. I've seen a jester. Over the years, I must have seen hundreds of them. They weren't always called jesters, you know—"

"I'm not asking if you've *ever* seen a jester! I'm asking if you've seen one in the past forty-eight hours."

"Forty-eight years?"

"Hours."

"Oh." Merlin grimaced. "That is a hard question. Let me think. Is it by any chance a trick? You two wouldn't happen to be jesters, would you? That would be entirely unfair. Though I imagine such a prank would be true to form for a pair of freelance jesters."

Emma reminded herself to keep a calm, even tone. "Do we look like jesters?"

"What do jesters look like?"

"Haven't you seen hundreds of them? They wear silly checkered costumes, with big jingling hats that look like upside down octopuses!"

"The plural of octopus is octopi."

"Have you seen one?"

"An octopus or a jester?"

"A jester!"

"No!"

Emma let out an enormous sigh. She closed her eyes and clenched her jaw. Merlin could be telling the truth. Sassy had only heard the jester mention Merlin's name. That didn't necessarily mean that he'd visited the wizard. But what *did* it mean?

"Unless…"

Emma was tired of being led down the garden path. If Merlin didn't pan out, then she didn't know where'd she go. But anything sounded better than listening to one more second of the wizard's voice. He had one more chance; then she was out of there. "Unless what?"

"Unless you mean the charming young man who dropped by yesterday morning."

"Can you tell me what he looked like?"

"Short fellow. Skinny, not too much meat on the bones, as they say. But no." Merlin shook his head. "He doesn't match the description you gave me. You see, he didn't wear checks."

"What was he wearing?"

"A rather garish green-and-white harlequin pattern. And his headpiece looked nothing like an octopus."

"What did it look like?"

"It didn't look like any sort of tentacled sea creature I know of. It only had four arms! Everyone knows an octopus has exactly eight."

Emma spoke through gritted teeth. "Did they have bells on them?"

"Yes."

"That's the jester!"

"Then yes, I saw him. He came by yesterday afternoon. Pleasant fellow. Rather fond of his puns, I'm afraid. Though he did tell me a very funny story about a giraffe who tried to perform a binding spell, except the giraffe was—unsurprisingly, I may say—not a very accomplished magician."

Emma's ears pricked up. The jester had spoken with

Merlin about the same type of spell that had kept Isolde's body in the human realm long enough to be discovered. "Tell me about the joke."

"I'm afraid the details are quite technical. You know, wizard humor."

"Try me."

"You see, the giraffe really was clueless. He flubbed the basic cantrips. Got his ley lines oriented backward, and in the end, he managed bind himself to the spot where he stood."

"You said it was a technical joke. Do you think the jester was a… wizard?"

"Far from it. While he might have parroted the basic form of the spell, he completely flubbed the details. And the details, as any wizard will tell you, are the most important part. He didn't even know that you could cast that spell on a coin and use it as a proxy. Otherwise, you'd have to convince your target to stay still for hours while you combined the necessary ingredients and chanted the necessary incantations."

"And I don't suppose you told him any of those ingredients or incantations?"

"I never would have. But the giraffe's spell was so fouled up I couldn't help but correct it."

"Did you give him a coin?"

"Don't be ridiculous. A proper proxy is far too valuable to give away."

"Did you sell him one?"

"One doesn't sell a priceless proxy for filthy lucre, mammon, mere money. And this jester fellow didn't have anything worth taking in trade. But he was so eager that I offered to show him a coin from my private collection that would be suitable for the enchantment." Merlin's words trailed off. He furrowed his brow and stared at the small gold coin in his wrinkled palm. "Now that you mention it, this coin does seem familiar. One moment." Merlin strode back behind the piles. Bottles and books and other unrecognizable things soon flew out from behind the pile, landing everywhere.

"Where did I put the blasted thing? Ah! There it is!" Merlin returned. He carried the enormous leather-bound book of coins which he'd proudly shown to them earlier that day. He thudded it onto the low table by the woodstove, cracked it open and began turning pages. "Here we are. Caesar Augustus— Why do I feel a sudden sense of déjà vu? All the way up to Caligula. Funny word, *Caligula*. In the present day, it carries connotations of violence, debauchery and excess. But if you spoke Latin you would know that it's the diminutive of the word *caliga*, which means *boot*. It was a nickname given to the future emperor as a child because he loved dressing up as a soldier. He would march around the palace in tiny combat boots." Merlin looked up at Emma. He seemed to want her to say something.

"That's… interesting?"

"Interesting? It's fascinating! Only, tell me now, why were we looking at my coin collection?"

"Cardamom."

"Yes! The giraffe! I understand you perfectly. I retrieved my coin collection because I wanted to see if"—he scanned the square coin pockets until his eyes came to rest on an empty one—"any of my Caligulas had gone missing. It appears that one has."

"It's in your hand."

"So it is! I must say, you're quite astute, Miss…"

"Emma."

"Well then, I suppose the coin was lost and found in the same hour. How fortunate."

"Except it wasn't lost," Emma said. "It was stolen. The jester tricked you into telling him the spells he needed, then stole the coin out from under your nose."

"The jester?" Merlin seemed perplexed. His mouth hung

open slightly, and his eyes seemed unfocused. Then a look of understanding spread across his features. He closed his mouth and set his jaw. His eyes came into focus.

He rose to his full height. His long hair and robe lifted subtly around him, as if billowed by an invisible wind. His skin seemed to glow with its own light. Even his beard changed from light gray to pure white. When he spoke, he was no longer an absent-minded old man. His voice boomed. "He tricked me? He stole my coin? What a jerk!"

"You tell 'em," Emma said.

"I'll see him hung from the tallest tower! I'll flay him alive! I'll make him watch while everything and everyone he loves burns to bitter ashes. I'll make his children and his children's children curse his name and rend their hair in lamentation that he ever darkened my doorstep and sought to match his wits against my own."

"No."

"What?" The wizard looked puzzled.

"No, you don't get to do any of that. This isn't the Dark Ages. King Arthur's long gone. We don't flay people. We don't hang them from towers. And if this guy even has kids, their lives are hard enough as it is. Besides, I have a thing against generational curses."

"What about snakes?"

"Excuse me?"

"Can I drop him into a hole full of snakes?"

"No!"

"You must be fun at parties." Merlin seemed hurt.

"Look," Emma said. "I'm sorry that he lied to you and stole from you. That must feel bad. I'd be upset too. But there's a lot more at stake here than your bruised ego. Isolde is dead. Killed, I assume, by the jester, who used your spells to bind her body to this realm. And that's not all. Sometime in the past couple of hours, Linda Cappotelli was killed."

"Was she? Oh, that's serious." But he didn't look like it

was serious. A sly grin spread across his face. "Terrible, really. Awful. If this jester did, indeed, kill Linda Cappotelli, then his days are numbered. The Cappotellis will punish him in ways more devious than anything I could devise."

Emma didn't love this attitude. But a win is a win. "You agree then. No flaying? No towers. No snakes?"

"A wizard does have a reputation to maintain." He spread his arms wide to encompass everything inside the tent: the stove, the chairs, the pile of old newspapers threatening to topple over at any moment. "All the wonders of the world might be found inside his workshop. If word gets out that he's unable to defend it from those who would rob him of his wonders, he might as well retire. So once in a very rare while, a little flaying might not be a bad idea."

"And here I thought you were just a cute old man."

"However, in these modern times, in this particular case, I think we can allow mercy to temper justice."

"How noble of you." Emma rolled her eyes. "Now tell me, do you remember the jester saying anything about why he wanted to see the coin or know about the binding? Did he mention that he worked with anyone? That he had any plans of any kind?"

"No."

"That's incredibly helpful. I guess the coin is yours. You'd better keep it."

"The coin? Oh yes." Merlin slid it into the empty pocket and closed his book. Sometime in the past few minutes, his beard had returned to its normal gray, and his skin once more showed its age. Merlin groaned a little as he hoisted the heavy book and trudged behind the junk piles to put it away.

Emma turned to Riley. "It's just so frustrating."

"I know. The way you looked at Merlin, I worried we were about to have a third murder on our hands."

"I don't mean Merlin. I mean the case."

"Isn't it going well?" Riley asked. "Merlin just tied the

coin to the jester. The coin had to be present at Isolde's murder. Therefore, he's linked the jester to the murder."

"You're right," Emma said, the frustration evident in her voice.

"Our evidence is more circumstantial with Linda's murder, but it's strong enough to give the cops. Even if you leave out all the magic stuff, the coin is a Cappotelli signature. The jester stole it from Merlin and left it with Isolde to frame Linda."

"Don't forget the dagger. It was covered in green gemstones arranged into the same triangle pattern on the jester's clothes."

"And the Fairykin were in conflict with the Cappotellis. They were trying to take over the black market."

"It all lines up. I see it. But something feels off. I can't believe that the Fairykin would kill Isolde. I mean, Ezell practically worshipped her. She started a fairy cult, for crying out loud."

"But they fought."

"Lots of people fight."

"Ezell acted upset when we asked her about the fight. What if she wasn't telling us the whole truth?"

Emma thought this over. "Do you mean that Isolde might not have agreed to stop the fairies' black market trade?"

"It's impossible to know. Our only source of information is Ezell, and it's impossible to corroborate her story. They might have argued about anything. Isolde might have rejected the Fairykin altogether."

"I still can't see Ezell murdering her idol."

"What about the others? The jester and that guy Brad might have gone behind her back."

"That must be it," Emma said. Doubt still nagged at her, but she forced herself to swallow it. "Once again, everything points to the jester in both cases. We've already put off reporting Linda's murder for too long. There's plenty of nonmagical evidence to give to the cops. It's not our crime to solve."

"What do we do? Call 911?" Riley asked.

"No. We'll report it to Griffin. This is his circus. He can handle the cops."

CHAPTER 21
DOUBLE CROSS

The darkened alley was eerily quiet now that most of the fairgoers had cleared out. In the distance above the tents, the Fairykin light show pulsed against low-lying clouds, lighting them from below like lightning. The thumping, grinding, earsplitting music was reduced by distance to the faintest thunder rumble. The kids seemed to like it. But that wasn't any normal party. It was a recruiting event. A shiver ran up Emma's spine. The jester, a likely killer, was over there. He had to be stopped.

She turned to Sassy, who sat on a low wall near Merlin's tent. "Did you run into any trouble out here?"

"Not a lick." He sounded disappointed.

"We're going to Griffin's office. I hope he's still here. We found out that the jester—"

"Let's go then." Sassy started walking. Emma and Riley rushed to keep up.

"Don't you want me to explain?"

"You don't have to. Remember? Cat ears?" To prove his point, Sassy swiveled his ears back and forth like miniature radar dishes. "You're going to have Griffin call the cops? You know they won't be able to do a thing about Isolde's murder.

If you told them the body disappeared as soon as you found it, they'd probably send you to the looney bin."

"I'll worry about that when it happens. If the jester killed Isolde, then Linda, what's stopping him from killing again? He didn't seem to think too highly of Ezell. Would she be next if she tried to stop whatever he was planning with the Fairykin?"

"Good points," Sassy said. "You remember your agreement with the fae? I'm the judge. I get to decide whether you've found Isolde's killer. From what I've seen, I think you've proven it. You've done your job. All we have to do is wait until the stroke of midnight, then tell Gresill that the jester's guilty. They'll take care of the punishment."

Emma's mouth hung open, and she stared at Sassy. He was right. She'd done her job. She felt all fizzy inside as she realized what this meant. She could go home and take off the ridiculous, heavy, itchy red coat. She could shower and put on pajamas and sit at her kitchen table with a cup of chamomile tea while she waited for the fae messenger to arrive. They'd give him the information, and if everything went smoothly, she'd have her dad back. This was what she'd dreamed of for as long as she could remember.

But what if she was wrong? Doubt, like an enormous black python, slithered around her stomach and squeezed. Sure, the jester looked guilty, but was she certain? Reporting him to the police would serve a purpose. It would get him off the streets, at least until he could post bail. If he was innocent, the truth would come out eventually.

But reporting him to the fae was a different story. She had no idea how they would punish him, but she doubted he'd receive a trial, let alone any chance to appeal. Emma sighed. Her limbs felt heavy. A cold feeling of resignation crept into her heart. "No, I'm not ready to say he's guilty beyond a shadow of a doubt."

"Are you sure?" Riley asked. "It seems like an open-and-shut case."

"Just trust me," Emma said. She wished she felt as confident as she sounded.

They arrived at Griffin's half-timbered office in the medieval cul-de-sac. Its lights still shone in the lattice windows, and a steady stream of smoke rose out of the chimney. It smelled like a campfire. Emma walked up to the heavy timber door and rapped her knuckles against the smooth wood. A moment later, the door swung open and a wave of heat rolled over Emma.

Griffin stood in the doorway, silhouetted against the fluorescent lights. He wore a white linen shirt unbuttoned to his sternum and rolled up at the sleeves. Beads of perspiration hung on his creased forehead. "I thought I told you I never wanted to see you again," Griffin said.

"Things changed," Emma said.

"Why am I not surprised? But a deal's a deal. If that's too hard for you, I could always have security escort you off the grounds." He paused long enough for that thought to sink in. "But I'll tell you what. Since I'm such a nice guy, I'm just going to shut my door and give you one more chance to live up to your end of our bargain and scram."

"Linda Cappotelli's dead."

Griffin staggered back. "Dead? How do you know?"

"We found her body in the time capsule pit. I did tell you that I'd leave you alone. I don't intend to break my promise. I just thought you'd want to know about the dead Mafia heiress on your property."

"No," he muttered. "You were right. This does change things."

"In that case, we have a pretty good suspect for you to report to the police."

Griffin glanced over his shoulder and frowned. "Well, I

guess you'd better come in and tell me everything you know."

Emma's shirt began to feel uncomfortably humid the moment she entered Griffin's office. The heat was overwhelming, even more so than Merlin's tent. The fireplace in the middle of the north wall blazed, sending crimson embers up the flue. It looked like it needed to be cleaned.

Emma walked past the cracked closet door and sat in one of the old wood-and-green-vinyl chairs in front of Griffin's massive desk. Riley sat in the other. Sassy had vanished. Someone had been tidying up since the last time they had been here. The piles of papers were gone from his desk, revealing a slick leather desk mat. Most of the old banker's boxes that had been piled around the desk were now flattened and leaned against the wall with other recyclables.

"So you think you know who killed Linda?"

"We have ideas."

"And you want me to communicate those ideas to the police? You do realize that they'll want to interview you."

"Fine with me," Emma said. "I'll leave my address and phone number." As soon as she said it, Emma wondered how comfortable she felt leaving that information with this stranger. It seemed like an invitation to get roped into other people's problems. Could she instead call the police in the morning and go in for an interview?

"Out with it then. Who killed her?"

Something about the way he leaned forward in his creaky chair pricked her intuition. She felt the hair on the back of her neck stand up. It would have been so easy to say, "The jester did it!" That's what she'd planned to say just a moment prior, but now? Riley glanced at her with a puzzled expression.

Emma forced herself to speak. "It all comes down to a coin which we found on Isolde's lips. We traced it…" There was that hesitation again. Some idea was trying to break through into her consciousness.

"Yes?" Griffin said. "Where did you trace it?"

A log popped in the fire, and she heard a sound like rustling leaves. She turned around to see that small black curls of ash had blown out of the fireplace onto the floor.

She knew.

She turned back to Griffin and, in a voice that was almost a whisper, said, "You did it."

The portly man paused, looking hard into Emma's eyes. Then a confused smile played over his face. "You're joking."

"I wish I was," Emma said. Her mind raced, weaving minute, seemingly inconsequential facts into a portrait of murder. "Let's start with the most obvious, glaring fact about Isolde's death. We found her inside a heavy concrete box, buried deep underground. It was located under the world tree. Anyone trying to dig it up would have expected to have to cut through at least some tree roots, yet the workers had no trouble excavating it by hand with shovels. This proves that ground had been dug before they got there."

"Of course somebody would have dug it up. How else would the body have gotten there? I don't know what it has to do with me."

"The easiest way to dig a hole like that, not to mention open a heavy concrete box, would be to use a backhoe. Heavy equipment like that leaves tracks in soft dirt. I happened to trip in one of those tracks by the world tree."

"Anyone could have brought equipment in through the woods at night."

"There's no need. You have a backhoe just down the road. I saw it being repaired. You told us earlier that you made your money as a general contractor. I'm sure if the police checked, they'd find that at some point in your life you were a licensed backhoe operator."

"So what? Half my crew knows how to run a backhoe."

"But you were the one with dirt under your fingernails. I saw you cleaning them earlier."

"That's your big reveal? Some lousy dirt?"

"No," Emma said. "My big reveal is those ashes around the fireplace. They look awfully like burned paper to me. It's cold outside, but not that cold. Certainly not cold enough to warrant such a huge fire, especially for someone sweating like you are."

"You're reaching."

"No, I'm betting. I'm betting that since the fire's still blazing, and since you didn't expect us to turn up, that you haven't finished destroying all the papers. I'd be curious to see inside your closet. I bet I'd find the contents of those ancient banker's boxes."

"And what do you imagine they contained?"

"Documents. Papers. Buried by the founders of the Emerald City Ren Faire. You told us that they ran out of money and sold the faire to you. But you were the reason they ran out of money. You were their contractor."

"The founders? They're ancient history. Why would I care about old papers?"

"You said it yourself. You spent a lot of money over a lot of years building up the myth of the founders. The crowds, the volunteers, all know the stories by heart. If they found out that you swindled the founders, the game would be up. You'd lose out on all the volunteer labor. People would go elsewhere."

"No offense, darling, but why don't you leave the investigation to the professionals? I'll call the cops. I'll even tell them your little story about the stolen coin."

Emma leaned in and looked Griffin in the eye. "How'd you know it was stolen?"

Griffin's eyes went wide with fear. He glanced toward the door, then to Emma and Riley, as if trying to determine if he could sprint out of there. But his sprinting days were long behind him. When he finally spoke, he sounded like a kid who'd been caught pinching cookies. "H-he made me do it!"

"Who?"

Griffin spoke in a whisper. "Aluicious! The one with the bells! The Fairykin!"

"Lies!" someone shouted behind them. Emma turned to see the closet door wide open. The jester stood in the doorway, his face lit up manically by the fire. He stepped forward. The bells on his headpiece jingled.

"Lookie what I found in your closet, little Rickie!" He swung his arm up. He held a dagger, long and silver. Green jewels peeked out from its handle. "Why would you have a duplicate of the weapon you killed that Cappotelli witch with?"

Richard Griffin didn't answer. He had risen from his chair and stood against the back wall, eyes fixed on the jester.

The jester took another step. *Jingle.*

"You told me that nobody'd ever trace the coin back to the wizard. You told me the Fairykin would have exclusive access to the black market. I should have known better. Tell me, were you always going to double-cross me?"

Jingle.

"Were you always going to kill Cappotelli and frame me? Tell everybody I made you do it? Pathetic!"

Jingle.

Griffin's face dripped with sweat as he panted. His eyes were wide with terror.

The jester pressed the dagger to his neck. "Little Rickie, tell me pretty, why should you own this place? Why should you have all the luck? Why should the rest of us bow and scrape for the scraps you throw us?"

Rickie didn't answer.

"I wonder what would happen if I killed you now? Would anybody care?"

No answer.

"If they did, would it be from love or because they believed the lies, the myths that you marketed to them?"

Suddenly a gust of cool wind entered the room. Ezell pushed through the front door, dragging a shame-faced Brad behind her. "And just what do you think you're doing?"

"Ezell?" The jester blinked and shook his head. "What are you doing here?"

"Brad told me everything. I... I can't believe it! I can't believe you literally killed Isolde! She was my friend!" Ezell strode over to the jester, snatched the dagger by its blade and threw it across the room. She kicked the jester in the shin and, when he bent over, walloped him on the back. "You are *so* kicked out of the Fairykin!" She glanced back. "Brad?"

"Yes, my queen?"

"Call the cops and make sure he stays down."

"Of course, my queen."

"Kick him if he moves."

"Where?"

"You know where."

CHAPTER 22
HEART

Emma used an oversized fork and spoon to scoop a generous helping of spaghetti a la Viv out of the enormous stainless steel pot onto her plate. The steam that rose above it filled the air with the aroma of sweet basil, pungent garlic, and earthy San Marzano tomatoes. She stepped to her right and picked up a Microplane and a block of parmesan cheese from the counter. She grated the cheese until her spaghetti looked like a peak in the snow-covered Alps. As she walked to her silverware drawer to get a fork, Emma glanced out of her kitchen window.

It was dark outside, spitting rain, and cold. So much could change in a day. In the weather, in life, in fortune. A day could see a wealthy land developer plucked from his land and tossed in a cell. It could see a fairy full of laughter turned into only a memory. It could assign a Mafia heiress to oblivion.

With so much darkness in the world, Emma's house seemed like a warm and cozy ship adrift on a wine-dark sea. She smiled. It was good to be home, even if the bills piled up and dishes needed doing.

Viv's big, booming laughter drifted into the kitchen from the dining room, along with clinks of silverware and glasses.

Emma tossed a slice of garlic bread onto her spaghetti mountain and went to join them.

So many people she cared about were packed around that table. Of course there was Viv, in a tank top and shorts despite the weather. She was deep in conversation with Riley. Jessie sat across from them in her chair, which was always pulled out in case the spirit wanted company. The other spirits, Rue, Bob, and Lily, preferred to hover discreetly in the corner of the room.

Viv looked up as Emma approached the table. "Riley said you met Merlin! Like, *the* Merlin?"

"Beats me." Emma pulled out her chair and sat. "I'm not surprised by anything at this point."

"And you talked your way into a rave? I didn't know you had it in you."

"They don't call them raves anymore," Jessie said wryly.

"I don't have it in me," Emma said. "We left as fast as humanly possible."

"There's just one thing I don't get," Viv said around a bite of pasta. "After the big fight when Sassy showed up with— What's his name? The fae in cat form."

"Gresill."

"More like grease-makes-me-ill. Am I right?" Viv waited for laughter that didn't come. "After he showed up, he said you won. You solved the murder."

"Yeah."

"But where's your dad?"

"I don't know." Emma let out a weary sigh. "I'm starting to wonder if maybe I missed something when I negotiated the deal with them. Maybe they tricked me."

"It seemed like you covered your bases to me," Riley offered.

"Thanks." Emma smiled sadly. She picked up her fork and twirled the spaghetti around it. She lifted it to her mouth and took a bite. She allowed herself to enjoy the savory, earthy tomato sauce seasoned with a handful of fresh basil and plenty of garlic. It warmed her and comforted her in a way that was both profound and familiar. It was the taste of home. Not some far-off homeland, but her home here with her friends. There was nothing fancy about spaghetti a la Viv, but it was perfect.

The doorbell rang.

"I'll get it," Emma said, rising from her chair. She wouldn't admit to herself that her heartbeat was rising. She wouldn't allow herself to be disappointed. The fae were tricksters, not to be trusted. The old floorboards creaked underfoot as Emma walked to the front door.

The window filling the door's upper half was covered by a solid white curtain. She saw the outline of a porch-lit figure on the other side. Could it be? Could it be everything she hoped for? Was this the moment she'd spent so many nights dreaming of when she was a child?

The polished brass door handle felt cold in her hand as she turned it. The door unlatched, shifting subtly toward her. She pulled it the rest of the way open.

Emma swallowed and tried to hide the tremor in her voice. "I've been expecting you."

The man standing on Emma's porch was short and stocky. He wore an immaculately tailored navy suit with a cherry-red tie. Enormous gold and diamond rings crusted his knuckles. When he spoke, his voice was gravely though not unfriendly. "I'm sorry to disturb your evening meal. But I believe you have an item of great sentimental importance to my family."

"I'm sorry for your loss." Emma offered him Linda's coin.

"Thank you." He sounded surprised.

"Are we all squared away now?" Emma asked.

"The Cappotelli family has no beef with you."

"I'm glad to hear it," Emma said. "Now if you'll excuse me, I'll get back to dinner."

"Of course, thank you."

Emma shut the door and leaned against it, slowly sinking to the floor. She wouldn't cry. She wouldn't admit that she'd gotten her hopes up. She wasn't—

"Hey, Em, everything okay?" Viv stood at the other end of the hall, looking at Emma. Her face was full of concern.

"No." Emma forced herself to stand.

"Wanna talk?"

"No. I want to finish dinner." Emma started toward the dining room, when suddenly the doorbell chimed again. She turned to see another porch-lit outline on the curtain.

Her vision narrowed, and her face flushed red with anger. She'd given back his stupid coin. What more did he want from her?

Who cared if he was a Cappotelli? She would tell that jerk exactly where he could go! Emma rushed back to the door and flung it open.

An older man stood on her porch. His messy gray hair curved down the sides of his face into sideburns, and he wore a disintegrating motorcycle jacket. Even in his advanced years, he looked just like the man in the photo on Emma's living room wall, a photo she didn't have to look at because she knew it by heart.

"Dad?"

NEXT IN SERIES:

Stitch Witch
Buy direct from the author at tabathagray.com

A hundred witches locked in a museum with a killer and the world's worst psychic. What could go wrong?

Life is good for Emma—well—except for the dad-shaped lump on her couch. Ever since he came back from the fae realm, he's been…different. It seems hopeless until a visitor arrives with a cure at a curious price. Emma must enter a magical sewing competition.

The Causeway Sewing Bee draws the best fabric artists from magical towns throughout the world. Emma may not know a cross stitch from CrossFit, but with a handy-dandy magic potion? It'll be a piece of cake… or not.

When stitches run red with murder, Emma must thread together the clues to catch the killer before they strike again.

But murder was only the beginning and witches' plans run deep. Whoever controls the sewing bee controls the fate of the witching world. Even as Emma closes in on the murderer, another hand prepares to strike…